# The Emperor's Body

Jan. 1998

To Dave and Val,

Speaking of fairy tales, you both may enjoy these. Maruyne Jenoff is my sister

On the occasion of Dave's sessions in Brandon, Manitoba at the AAFC Research Centre there.

Carol Enns
(Library and Information Centre Manager)

# The Emperor's Body

Marvyne Jenoff

*Paintings by Miles Lowry*

Ekstasis Editions

Canadian Cataloguing in Publication Data

Jenoff, Marvyne
    The emperor's body


    ISBN 0-921215-80-0

    I. Title.
    PS8569.E57E46   1995    C813'.54        C95-910586-4
    PR9199.3.J46E46   1995

Acknowledgements:
    Some of these stories have appeared, in slightly different form, as follows: *Pygmalia* in *Paperplates*, *Hansel* in *Canadian Woman Studies*, *Sat On a Wall* in *Other Voices* and *Paperplates*, *The Youth And The Sun* (as *The Sun*) in *Prism International*, *The Beanstalk, Et Al.* in *Canadian Woman Studies*, *Chicken Little*, *The Prophet* in *Paperplates*, *The Hare, The Tortoise, And The Human Race* on CBC Radio, *Cloud Nine*, *The Possible Cheese* in *Mother Tongues*, *The Sprats' Spat* in *The Antigonish Review*, *Cinderella And All The Slippers: The Story Of The Story* in *The Fiddlehead*
    For editorial and personal support, I would like to thank: Carol Enns, Linda Gibson, Iris Horowitz, Harry Howith, Francis Landy, Margot Matthews, Jill Mayer, Irene McGuire, Varda Horowitz Wilensky, and, especially, Leona Wiebe Gislason.
    The epigraph is loosely adapted from *Ivar's Story*, a medieval Icelandic legend, in *Hrafinkel's Saga and Other Stories*, translated by Hermann Palsson, Penguin Classics, 1971, reprinted in 1977.

Published in 1995 by
**Ekstasis Editions Canada Ltd.**                   **Ekstasis Editions**
Box 8474, Main Postal Outlet                               Box 571
Victoria, B.C. V8W 3S1                         Banff, Alberta T0L 0C0

*The Emperor's Body* has been published with the assistance of a grant from the Canada Council and the Cultural Services Branch of British Columbia.

Printed and bound in Canada by Hignell Printing Ltd.

# Contents

**I**

1. Pygmalia     13

2. Hansel     15

3. Sat On A Wall     19

4. The Youth And The Sun     23

5. The Beanstalk, Et Al.     27

6. The Emperor's Body     33

**II**

7. The Fox, The Grapes, And The Author     49

8. Chicken Little, The Prophet     53

9. The Hare, The Tortoise, And The Human Race     63

10. The Possible Cheese     69

11. The Sprats' Spat     73

12. *Twinkle, Twinkle, Little Star*, The International Anthem     79

**III**

13. Cinderella And All The Slippers: The Story Of The Story 85

*To Joan Bodger Mercer, forerunner,*
*and in memory of Margot Matthews, 1942-1995*

The King tried to comfort the poet, who had been betrayed in love.

The King suggested other women, but the poet replied they would only remind him of his beloved. The King offered money for travel or estates to manage, but the poet was not tempted.

At last the King suggested, *If you like, on quiet evenings, come sit by me. Then you can tell your story as many times as you wish, and I will listen.*

*Icelandic legend*

I

# *Pygmalia*

A rolling stone once followed a sculptress. Admiring her stride it rolled along behind her to her garden. There, warmed by her attention, it was content to stay.

The sculptress studied the shape of the stone from different perspectives. With her hands she learned its smoothness. Timidly at first, she carved designs on it. Then boldly she carved her name on it, for what is safer than stone?

She spoke to the stone, and its silence distressed her. She longed for it to reply but, being stone, it said nothing. She stroked the stone, she lay with her ear pressed gently to it. Perhaps she could coax some response. But it made no sound. She kicked the stone. She kicked it over and over. And the stone began to roll again.

As it made its way slowly along the road, passers-by admired the stone with its designs and brought their friends to see it. They read the sculptress's name and she became famous, though that wasn't what she wanted, alone in her garden.

When the stone rested near its fellows in the graveyard, people read her name and thought she was dead. That wasn't what she wanted either, tormented in her garden.

# *Hansel*

The witch lived at the edge of the multicoloured city, where things happened. She lived in the kind of building where she wasn't allowed to display anything on the outside. So when she felt lonely she wore her gingerbread on her sleeve, conjured up some candy-coloured tickets, and took the train into the city like everyone else.

There was a boy, new to the city. Stopped at a traffic light, uneasy in the crowd, he found himself absently eating gingerbread delicious beyond belief. He was just about to eat the sleeve, as well, when he remembered his manners. He introduced himself. He complimented the witch on her gingerbread. He asked whether she also made shortbread and macaroons and jelly beans and licorice sticks. How wonderful to be able to make all those things! He admired the witch herself, and asked wistfully where she lived.

The witch felt lonelier than ever. Aware of how quickly her future was approaching, she proposed a bargain. *Come home with me,* she said. *I will teach you all I know, if you will stay with me when I am dying.*

So the boy lived in the apartment with the witch, and there were always wonderful smells from the oven. As long as he listened well and wanted to be like her, the witch was happy. In love she became less of a witch and was glad of the change. She forgot how to conjure up train tickets. She no longer bothered to bake. When the boy took over her kitchen she was proud of him.

She praised his work and he learned quickly. He willingly shaped his hands to her eccentric utensils. Gracefully he bent to reach the low oven. But when he found himself making up his own recipes, her utensils no longer fit his hands and broke in use. He began to feel caged in. And when he suspected she was praising him indiscriminately, he felt he was being held for some sinister purpose. One day, head full of recipes, no thought of the train, the boy walked back into the city.

She is old now. Most days she is content to watch TV with the neighbours, nibble chocolate from the convenience store, and

15

dream about her gingerbread man, for by now he is surely a man. She likes to imagine him striding through the city, making things happen.

When she thinks of dying she remembers their bargain. She is enough of a non-witch now to admit it was probably unfair. He was only a boy at the time, sweet thing, too young to understand.

She often thinks of dying. She would like him to visit just once, though she doesn't suppose he will.

But some days she wakes up a witch again. Enough of a witch to say, a bargain is a bargain. She walks and plots, morning and evening, refusing to die.

# Sat On A Wall

When you see an egg sitting on a wall you can be sure it knows how to keep its balance.

Once, in a land of no king and no king's men, where horses belonged to whomever they pleased, a large, well-formed egg propelled herself by means of her long skirts through the town as she went looking for a wall. She chose a low wall that surrounded a flower-bed on the main street not far from the lake. On top of the wall there was a comfortable-looking indentation, where a few bricks were lower than the ones around them. Using her skirts the egg hoisted herself up and settled into her chosen spot. There with the help of a wide-brimmed hat she maintained her balance. Perfect and proud she sat there, claiming kinship with the other balancing things nearby, the bicycles on the street, the sailboats on the lake, the clouds in the sky, and the sky itself.

In this land there was a lone prince who was and was not looking for a dragon. He needed a dragon to tame and learn from, so that afterwards he would know how to love a princess. He had heard of princes who hunted and killed dragons. He hoped there were no such princes in the town—he certainly didn't want to run into a dragon who expected a fight. Thus, looking for a dragon and hoping he wouldn't find one, the prince was startled by the sight of the well-dressed egg sitting pale and balanced on a wall. Overcome by a rush of trust, harmony, and intimations of wonderful things about to begin, he bowed to the egg.

*O Gracious Roundness*, he addressed her. *You are my dragon and my princess. I will love you all my days if you will only covet what I covet, blame what I blame, and pay attention to me every moment.*

In this innocent proposal the prince revealed the nature of all princes, who are bred, if not to conquer worlds, at least to be quoted in the newspaper. But the egg, according to her nature, would not hear anything that might disturb her balance. There is a reason why eggs have shells. She allowed herself to hear the prince speak of love.

19

Indeed, whether she would have allowed it or not, there was a great surge in her heart when he spoke so. The egg dearly wished the prince would come up onto the wall and sit beside her. Then she would draw his youthful spirit in towards her heart, and she and her prince would become one shell. Since she had such an attractive, serviceable shell, they would become *her* shell. As for paying attention to him every moment, she had begun to do so as soon as she saw how he looked at her and realized he was no ordinary prince.

The prince bowed once more before the egg, and the egg, inspired, inclined toward the prince. Respectfully he climbed up beside her. At first he sat very still and whispered to her. When he spoke of love, when he praised her, when he told her his boyish dreams, she replied with subtle motions. He could feel his spirit being drawn in through the pores of her shell and mingling with the mystery that radiated out. He grew bolder. He loved to stroke the egg's pebbled surface, and she, longing to bend further toward the sweetness of his touch, learned from the bicycles on the street how to balance in motion. Animated by his presence, she balanced with daring and exhilaration. She executed little hops and pirouettes, so joyful was she. And the boats and bicycles learned from the egg, and there was happiness in the land.

But when the prince spoke once more of coveting and blaming, the egg, with a serious rearrangement of her skirts, straightened up from his embrace. The more he spoke of such things, the more she had to pay attention to keeping her balance. Sometimes he wondered whether the egg knew he was there beside her, so still was she. He began to doubt her love. He missed her carefree movements. If only she would look at him! If only she would let him cherish her, hold her till she thought as he did! But the egg stayed self-possessed. She would allow nothing into her shell but praise.

He dreamed of yin and yang, himself the powerful black fish, infusing her with his need, fusing them together in one endless motion. But by then the egg could sense his dreams, and he woke to that deflecting movement of her shoulder, subtle as only an egg could suggest. He dreamed of iridescent dragons, twisting and self-absorbed, himself a unicorn with golden prize held high, unable to move or speak. And he woke to the shock of the egg's poised paleness. He dreamed he was the softest rain, the kind that would

20

gently make its way beneath the grass, but the spinning earth flung the rain off in tangents. When he woke from this dream, the prince, with whatever spirit he had left, stole away across the flower-bed into the night.

The egg chose not to pay attention to his leaving. She was still immersed in her displeasure at his dreams. She forgot she and her prince had ever loved. She didn't realize their love had changed her. But she needed his presence now to maintain her balance. Her wide-brimmed hat inclined toward the prince's space, but the egg inclined the other way. Bicycling in her sleep, not knowing what felt wrong, the egg toppled from the wall. There she lay on the pavement, tangled skirts, large shards of shell, and the huge yellow heart exposed and flat, in a land of no king, no king's men, and the prince gone hunting.

# The Youth And The Sun

Icarus liked his father's workshop well enough, with its models of castles, ports, and labyrinths. He could make a thing or two himself. But no way was he going to follow in the old man's footsteps. Instead, he followed the sun and came upon an old woman with a similar workshop, where he felt at home.

She wasn't that old a woman, he saw when he looked again. She was an inventor of ornaments, toys, and other fancies. He liked to stand in the yard near her doorway and watch her work. With old friends visiting often she had never really paid attention to youth. She had a candy ready in her hand—that's what she gave to children when it was time for them to go home—when she noticed that he was not so young.

Icarus saw the candy and ran away to hide his face. Then, when he was ready, he brought flowers and planted them in the yard. He brought a goat and milked it for her. He brought her honey in the comb.

All the while she was forging something on her anvil. A trapeze, perhaps, a firefly cage, or part of a new toy she called an airplane, that worked with a rubber band. She knew he was watching. She wielded her hammer more extravagantly, showing her strength, showing the different sounds she could make. Exultantly into the night she forged, and the glow, like a sun contained, drew Icarus closer.

She stopped her work. She touched his skin. And at the table where she worked with soft things—mushrooms, bubbles—out of tiny feathers and wax from the honeycomb she made him a little pair of ornamental wings.

Talking, they shared their passion for the sun and embraced in a solemn pact to honour it. They would make wings for each other, real ones they could fly with. Together they would build a high tower and jump from the top; buoyant, building momentum, they would soar to the sun and bow before it hand in hand.

23

Sun in their hearts, they hid the wings as they worked on them. At midday they would walk, showing each other off in the full light. They wore brighter and brighter colours. They devised daring physical feats they might use for flying and practiced openly. Icarus was proud for he had aimed high, a woman old enough to know everything but not too old. And she enjoyed her good fortune, a high-spirited youth intelligent enough to appreciate her. Their separate friends, skeptical at first, in time agreed with them.

Icarus finished her wings. He presented them wrapped in paper he had decorated himself. The wings, too, had a naive look to them. She felt shy. Would their sweetness suit her? When she tried them on they pressed against her neck. A rough part irritated the skin on her ribs. And she feared they were unsafe. She suggested how he might fix them. She could show him how to align them better, how to smooth them. Tactful as she thought she was, Icarus was hurt to tears so she hugged him and said no more. After that it took her a very long time to finish his wings. They needed only the strongest and largest feathers for serious flight. But she sat sullen at her table, not working, and he skirted around the workshop, not daring to disturb her, not daring to hint.

And so the tower became their focus. They drew plans, always happy to compromise, laughing at their preposterous suggestions. They brought home samples of what they might use to build it, bricks in rainbow colours, mortar made of sugar, petals, cobwebs. They found books and studied comparative towers. They talked of travelling to observe towers under different conditions of light and in different seasons. They talked about every possible and impossible detail of their tower. And they dreamed about talking about the tower.

They often went out to look for a building site but they never got very far. They would put on their wings, hers ill-fitting, his unfinished, and fly around a little, sometimes as high as a cottage roof, but, heavy with what remained unsaid, they flew mostly nearer the ground. Having to concentrate on flying, they couldn't talk much. And in their silence, in the failure of their wings, at last they were able to feel despair. Their friends gathered at the shores of separate seas.

The tower was never begun. For, one day as they were flying they shouted at the same time, *Why don't you finish/fix my wings?* But they didn't hear each other. Their words collided in the air, and the force of their breath propelled them in opposite directions. Separate winds bore them over the heads of their friends and released them into the water.

This is not a grand tragedy, at least not at this point. Since they never managed to get very far up, they did not fall with much force, nor did they plunge dangerously deep. Their friends easily pulled them out and dried them off.

The woman retreated to her workshop, where she nursed her embarrassment for a time. Then she resumed her work. At first she thought of him in anger and made fireworks, each more like the sun. She called them Atomic, Hydrogen, and Neutron. Then, remembering him with joy she made little towers in glass and filigree to catch the sunlight. She called them Babel, Eiffel, CN. And so the woman lived out her days.

Icarus felt contempt for what she was doing. Did she really think such tokens honoured the sun? He would do better than that. Fired with his plan Icarus returned to his father's workshop, prepared to learn this time from someone he could trust. Real wings, a real tower, these were his life. No more romantic notions of approaching the sun hand in hand. This time he would go alone and look the sun in the eye.

His father, alarmed, made wings for himself and joined him. But Icarus got away. When they jumped from the tower Icarus soared straight up. The heat of the sun softened the wax in his wings. The wind dislodged the feathers. Icarus wondered, *Why did the sun do that? Is it shocked by my audacity? Jealous that I've come so high? Is it careless in its loneliness? Next time I'll use platinum, acrylic, teflon,* he said to himself as he fell to his death in the sea.

The woman's death was not remarkable. Her name is not remembered, though many of her fancies survive in some form. The death of Icarus is documented, contemplated, honoured in art. Sweet youth naked in the air, puzzled by feathers, he is loved for the innocence of his folly.

# *The Beanstalk, Et Al.*

Jack leaped so high as he hacked down the beanstalk that the remaining stump reached well above his head. Then kicking at the fallen giant to make sure he was dead, he flung down his axe and ran off to find a girlfriend he could boast to. He brought her back to the stump of the beanstalk. There in the shelter of the few remaining leaves he built them a simple house.

The giant's widow looked down through the hole in her cloud where the beanstalk had been, and she did not like what she saw. Outside the little house were displayed the bag of gold, the hen that laid the golden eggs, and the golden harp, which Jack had stolen from the giants' house. And there stood Jack in front of his girlfriend and a few passers-by, gesturing with his arms wide, as if boasting about a fish he had caught.

Mrs. Giant could have killed them in one swoop. She could have let herself drop down through the hole in the cloud and landed on them and their house. But she didn't. For by killing something so small, the principle went, she would become small herself. By a similar principle, a giant-killer takes on giant-like qualities. Mrs. G. decided to wait until Jack became a worthy opponent.

She was also curious to see which of her husband's qualities Jack would manifest, and what sort of man he would become. Jack was the only boy who had visited them three times, and she had grown fond of his courageous spirit. She remembered how they had giggled together before her husband came in, and how Jack grinned from his hiding-place behind the stove as she discreetly passed him bits of her dinner. Finally, embarrassed at dwelling on Jack, Mrs. G. pulled herself together the only way she could, by remembering how Jack had robbed them and killed the giant. She proceeded to grieve for her husband and set the record straight about him.

People who know the story from the conventional point of view have no idea what life on the cloud was really like. They seem to think the giant was uncouth, but Mrs. G. had only to frown with disapproval, or be about to frown, and he would immediately remember his manners and shower attention on her. It is true that the giant had a taste for boys. Perhaps because of this his enthusiasm is mistaken for crudeness. People generally think the giant was greedy, that he counted and re-counted his gold coins, waking the world with wanton thunder. But that wasn't it at all. For she and her husband, in their giants' quest for knowledge, had arranged and rearranged the coins to illustrate their flights into higher mathematics. The hen that laid the golden eggs was the result of the giants' patient and affectionate breeding. Their next plan was to produce hens with moral qualities. As for the golden harp, of course it had cried out *Master* when Jack was stealing it. The harp, which the giants had created together in their early love, had been their companion, and when the three of them sang together they produced what came to be known as the music of the spheres. And Mrs. G. had a personal mission, to take care of the boys who visited the cloud. She was able to save almost every one. For she had only to pout, or be about to pout, and the giant would forget the meal he was planning and have eyes only for his wife. Her husband provided all the attention she asked for. The only person who ever paid more attention to her, with no effort on her part, was Jack. And she remembered her fondness for Jack, and her anger at his betrayal.

With appropriately vengeful feelings Mrs. G. looked down once again from her cloud. This time she was gratified to see what was happening at Jack's house, and she watched for a long time. The gold coins sounded flat as Jack counted them. Not recognizing their talents, he spent them one by one. By the time the coins were gone the gold standard had been replaced by the air and water standard. The golden eggs, beautiful as they were, became worthless in the conventional sense, and Jack and his girlfriend used them for food. The harp, so long away from expert hands, lost its tune and quarrelled with the hen. Against this cacophony, Jack and his girlfriend walked out of step with each other. And that was fine with Mrs. G.

As she continued to look down she noticed something that Jack and his girlfriend were not aware of. She saw the beanstalk growing again from the old stump, and she decided that was how she would descend for the kill. She would wait until the beanstalk reached her cloud, for as yet Jack had shown no sign of acquiring giant-like qualities. She would step down the leaves majestically, as befit a person of her stature. She planned what she might wear.

The beanstalk was determined to grow cautiously this time. The first time it had sprouted from its magic bean and grown right up to the clouds in one night, a night that heaved the earth and Jack with it. But having been so brutally felled the beanstalk had second thoughts about its youthful impetuosity. This time it wanted to be a tree, or at least as sturdy as a tree, to withstand any weapon and any man. So the beanstalk took its time. And with a giant's patience, Mrs. G. waited.

As she sat sewing with her golden darning egg she contemplated her new life on the cloud. With the abundance of air and water she was rich, according to the current standard. Now that flesh-eating was out of fashion and not mentioned, Mrs. G. was no longer embarrassed by her husband's tastes. She invented games of solitaire with the remaining gold coins and enjoyed their musical sounds as she handled them. To this counterpoint she often sang, songs she had once sung with her husband and their harp, then songs of her own. The hens that remained on the cloud laid eggs in a whole spectrum of colours, a wealth of choice before her breakfast.

When the beanstalk reached the cloud, the boys she had saved, who had heard of the giant's death, climbed up to visit her. They were men now. Some came with their girlfriends or families. Some came by themselves and stayed awhile. No longer anxious for their welfare, Mrs. G. was able to relax in their company and bask in her accomplished mission.

Her new mission was to keep the air and water fresh and justly circulating. Esthetes came to experience at source their refined pleasures of breathing and slaking thirst. Scientists and politicians, coming to learn her methods, stayed to learn also from the esthetes. Some stayed for the pleasure of their hostess's company. And so Ms G., as she now called herself, who had once mourned the golden age of her married life, bloomed differently in the heavenly age she was experiencing now. She found she would rather procrastinate thus than bother about Jack and his girlfriend.

In fact, it wasn't until her visitors stopped coming that she was curious enough to look down once more through the old beanstalk-hole in the cloud. When she saw the mass of leaves beneath her she understood what had happened. The beanstalk had turned itself into a new species that defied classification. It produced no beans, but that didn't matter. For it had grown into the tallest free-standing organism in the world, a great, tree-like thing, so strong and spread out at the top that it had lifted the entire cloud higher than anyone could climb. It had certainly grown past the point where Ms G. would have been able to step down.

At first she was angry. She thought, *No beanstalk is going to get the better of me. I can still fall on them.* But she remembered the principle that if you go far to kill something, you can never return the same. And there was no way Ms G. was going to change anything she had or anything she was. She looked around her, seeing her cloud anew. She saw the intricate carpet of beanstalk leaves making her cloudpath firmer, supporting her at higher and higher altitudes in the slow walk of her contentment, in the heaviness of her age.

When she looked down from this new height she could barely see the couple. But there seemed to be more animals in their yard, more people, perhaps children. The whole yard had a golden look—were there that many eggs now? Jack and his girlfriend, going about their daily business, seemed to walk in step, now lively, now peaceful. Ms G. thought she could hear their rhythms echoed by the golden harp, and that was fine.

The beanstalk continues to lift the cloud. The higher Ms G. gets, the less she sees and the more she seems to know. She is much less interested in Jack now, though pleased with what he has become. He has not increased much in stature, he does not bear much resemblance to the giant, but he has grown into a different kind of man, the kind who cook vegetables and remember folktales. As for his girlfriend, Ms G. waxes eloquent here. For Jack's girlfriend has grown into the image of Ms G. in her youth, a beauty, though of course much less impressive in size. How purely she sings, how gracefully she bends, as she goes about her woman's work! And look, there she is now, beginning to write a woman's story.

# The Emperor's Body

He woke bewildered from a dream. He who had discovered how not to dream and had been taking advantage of that discovery for some time. An impression of watery green stayed with him.

From the spacious bed he looked up through the east window at the mountain, Historical Mountain, with the light starting behind it. At its peak his ancestors had begun their Empire. In its shadow lay the city, Essential City, all that remained after a long history of conquering territories and releasing them.

He, himself, in his seaside palace, was the Silent Emperor, His Embodiment of Adornment. *Adornment* because, though his ancestors were known for their clothes, clothes were all that had made his position bearable when he was young. *Silent* because, well into his reign, he realized with joy there was nothing more he needed to say. Now, he had discovered, he didn't even need to dream. Sitting up, he looked through the west window over the sea, the Evermore Sea, and forgot himself.

Until he heard the Ministers rustling outside his door. A new outfit must be waiting. Intimations of his old, inherited duty came back to him. Stronger than the instincts to be calm and reflect and to ignore everything else, so strong he felt the Empire depended on it, was the duty to appear regularly before the citizens and show himself clothed. At first he had felt foolish standing there being looked at. He preferred walking. The Ministers and courtiers started out with him, and, as he walked through the city, the townspeople and their children followed. Thus the Emperor and all his citizens formed a procession. In time, it became a regular procession to the foot of the mountain. To the foot of the north slope, with its wind and its scent of sacredness. Then a procession with a purpose, a ceremony for the remembrance of the Emperor's ancestors, as if bringing the pleasure of clothing back to them and laying it at their feet.

It was summer. It was time. Today he would lead a

33

procession. He adjusted his morning-robe with its deep hood and folded his hands in the sleeves. Through the distances luxury afforded, with the slowness dignity demanded, he padded in his slipper-socks toward the Imperial dressing chamber. He recalled his favourite historical dreams, which she later expressed in his clothes, his stoic dream, standing rock-like as the swirling snow clung to him in sculpted shapes, and his fierce dream, arms upstretched to display the length of eagle feathers. His recent dreams were quieter, expressing seasons, the seasons here at the seaside expressing merely esthetic differences. And his new dream, that did not seem to be his own, came back to him. He was playing in the sea, concealed just under the greenish surface of its spreading waters, made languid by the waters, drawn out only by the desire to see the clothes she had laid out for him.

In front of the dressing chamber courtiers fawned. He shut the door against them. There were the clothes, all different shimmering colours, all green at the same time, like summer light glinting through water. He lifted the inner garments, amazed at their barely-perceptible weight. In a slow, private ritual he put them on. The robe was heavy, the hem blue as the depths of the sea. Light as haze was the crown-like headgear, silk swirling down from it as from the silvery gloves. He admired himself in one mirror after another around the room until he looked out the west window over the sea and stood there forgetting himself.


A little way up the west slope of the mountain, looking over the city, the palace, and the sea, the Minister of Adornment sat on the porch of her studio, waiting for the procession. Waiting for the sight of the Emperor in his new, summer clothes to assure her she had done the right thing. For this outfit had originated in an unusual way. Gone was the familiar rhythm, the Emperor dreaming in his palace and she waking in the mountain studio inspired with the beginnings of his next outfit. His dream for spring had eluded her. Not sure whether he had dreamed of clouds or apple-blossoms, she had made the clothes so light, even the headgear—was it a faintly-coloured calyx or a fan of sunbeams swooping down over his face to his shoulders—that he was almost lifted away by the north-slope wind. After that he hadn't dreamed at all, as far as she could tell. What was she to do? As sure as her instincts for creating, and for walking to reflect on her work, was her inherited duty to keep the Emperor clothed. The dignity of the Empire depended on it.

34

As did the spirit of the citizens. From her weaver ancestors she had learned the history of fashion. How, living on the mountain and having to dress for the demands of each season, the citizens developed the need for variety, then for art. What others were wearing became important, as did the need to outdo them. This was the age of wars. Gradually, along with the Imperial spirit, the citizens mellowed with the milder seasons toward the foot of the mountain and then toward the sea. Townspeople, courtiers, Ministers, all dressed plainly now, their vestigial creative needs fulfilled by the Emperor's new outfit as they walked in step with him in procession. All this depended on her work.

As did her own well-being. While she had waited in vain for some indication of the Emperor's summer dream, her hands, unused to idleness, chose silks of their own accord. She let these be her inspiration. Weaving the sea-like colours, she created a dream and wished it for him. She sewed pebbles into the hem of the robe to keep him in touch with the ground. Then, as she always did, she carried the outfit silently through the dark city, as the townspeople turned in their sleep, eager to behold the Emperor's new clothes in the morning light.

Now, anxious in the light of noon, she missed her fellow Ministers. She saw them, needed to see them, only at processions. But her missing them now took her back to the years when her studio was in the palace and they all worked in awareness of each other. The Minister of Finance designed colourful currency to attract colourful cargoes, though even then the citizens preferred what they found at home, enjoying money for its look and feel and historical value. The Minister of Air Traffic kept the air free of subterfuge and sarcasm, though no one remembered what those meant, and plotted to intercede with falling stars on behalf of the citizens in the days when there were wishes. Under the Ministers' care the city had thrived, and a soft silence enveloped the Emperor and themselves.

She looked back to that early silence. How it had heightened her nearness to the Emperor! Though they never spoke, they listened for each other's sounds, though they looked away, each mirrored the other's movements. And their silent play, who was the more vain, who could ignore the worse faults, who was quicker to pick up the other's incipient thoughts? When at last they chose to see they were not really keeping the spirit of silence, she designed a new studio beyond the outskirts of the city, on the west slope of the mountain. By then her hands had been so shaped by her work that whatever she made fit the Emperor and expressed him. As he entered further into silence she added headgear, sometimes with a veil or a mask, though it pained her to cover that face.


Quarrelling near the studio on their inherited park benches were the two men known as swindlers. At her work she often heard them through her windows. As if her silence meant she couldn't hear them, they spoke openly. They kept trying to figure out why they had been given a bad name for nothing worse than idling on park benches rather than indoors. Furthermore they had a persistent inkling that the Emperor was hiding something under his clothes. They could see the clothes, but they couldn't see the Emperor. This was as far as they usually got before the procession drew them in. But in this morning's long delay their quarrelling escalated, prickling with new ideas. Could it be that along with their name went an inherited duty, to expose the Emperor? Inspired at last with a purpose, they left quickly toward the south.

She laughed at their scrappiness. How long since she had laughed? She was annoyed to feel threatened by their purpose. And relieved that these malcontents had left the Empire. All these unfamiliar feelings disturbed her, for so long she had been either lulled or made proud by her work. And she would miss the swindlers, their voices the most frequent human sounds she heard. Ashamed of her pettiness, she covered her face with her hands.

And kept them there, ashamed that her feelings might have been seen. For beyond the swindlers' empty benches, waiting in front of the little house where he lived, stood the youth. No one knew where he had come from. But as she went walking around the foot of the south slope she had caught glimpses of him building his house, or the few scaled-down experimental shelters he had made beforehand. She had seen him running and jumping on the slope, attempting joy. Now she felt she shared his sadness. She wanted to see the details of his work. She might have gone to his house. She might have spoken to him.

But she was a Minister. Her silence, which kept her attuned to the Emperor, was central to her position. She stood up and turned the other way. And almost upon her was the procession. The Emperor's clothes flowed as she had designed them to flow. He walked at a leisurely pace, Ministers and courtiers around him, followed by the townspeople from their kitchens and workshops. Animated by the Emperor's presence, many exaggerated his movements in a languorous dance. At the edges of the procession

36

children waving ribbons or sparklers played in wider and wider circles. Their laughter cheered her. Her fellow Ministers swerved from their path to enfold her, acknowledging her role in the fragile normality of the day. Eyes stinging, she let their welcome soothe her as best she could.


At the site of the ceremony, at the north foot of the mountain, the citizens were relieved to take their familiar places. Strong as their instincts to greet their neighbours and do as they did was their inherited duty to behold the Emperor in his clothes. The steadfastness of the Empire depended on it. They braced themselves in the stirring wind, so like the winds that must have inspired their ancestors. During the spring ceremony they had feared the wind would lift the Emperor in his cloud-petal outfit, lift, perhaps scatter, them all. But now the Emperor stood firm, and they watched his summer sea-clothes furl in the wind, shade upon shade of hidden under-colour revealed until, primed by the experience of beauty, the citizens were ready.

The Minister of Eloquence, who had evolved throat-clearing to the highest art, commanded attention and intoned the titles: Emperor of the High Peak, Emperor of the Sharp Peak, Emperor of Blood in the Snow. The very sound of the names recalled the time when the fur-clad Emperors high on the mountain, surveying the distant east, planned defences of the territories they held and those they intended to hold. Over time, responsibility for outlying territories became burdensome, and peace was seen in a favourable light. The Emperor of Clinging in the Wind moved the palace part-way down the milder, west slope of the mountain, releasing the territories he could no longer see. In the time of the Emperor of the Cozy Crevice, the first to replace boots with slippers, the beginnings of a town gathered around the palace. Under subsequent Emperors the town followed the palace further down to where sheep lived, and hunters became shepherds and then weavers. In this milder climate toward the foot of the mountain the citizens were able to grow food rather than having to take it in battle, and the population increased without the help of captives. The town grew into a city, Essential City, which followed the palace right down the mountain to the edge of the sea. The citizens enjoyed the beach, and there flourished a long, uneventful dynasty characterized by reflection: The Emperor of One Toe in the Water, the Emperor of

Two Toes in the Water, the Emperor of Three Toes in the Water, and so on, to the twin Emperors, Their Majesties of Infinity and Grain of Sand. In the same tradition, standing before them now, was the Silent Emperor, his Embodiment of Adornment.

After the litany came the familiar reverberation and the welcome contemplative stillness. An anxious stillness this time, lengthened almost past endurance by the Emperor's distractedness. Until he slowly turned toward the city and started back, the courtiers prancing in his wake.

The Ministers, who were usually seen fleeting through the palace if they were seen at all, stayed to enjoy the work they had been planning. The townspeople had looked forward to working with them. The Minister of Roads held marathon walks to tamp down irregularities in the pavement and encourage the wind to blow the dust off the streets, though these tasks were done more out of tradition than of need. The Minister of the Environment went down to the edge of the sea, where he orchestrated the water and the weather, as his assistants looked in vain for litter so they could tidy the beach. The Minister of Agriculture walked in the fields. From the fragrance of the soil she was able to tell which crops would produce gentleness in whoever ate them, though by now this quality was widespread. She and her assistants gathered the vegetables waiting in the fields, scooped up the kernels of grain that had fallen in convenient piles, and turned the cheeses ripening in their forms among the buttercups. Through these tasks the Imperial spirit spread from its origins in the palace, the Emperor's calm, echoed and kept buoyant by the Ministers' silence, the Ministers themselves sustained by their nearness to each other.

The Minister of Adornment watched from her porch, and the youth, from one of the swindlers' benches, watched with her. Her own assistants collected materials, strands of wool which their sheep had moulted among the flowers and the breezes had gradually spun, extra filaments their silkworms had lavished into the harmonious air, filaments that glistened round the bushes and took on the colours of twigs, leaves, and sunshine. These materials they left on the porch of her studio. Then they returned to their homes at the outskirts of the city, where they wove the cotton that grew in their yards. Wove for their families, who sustained them.

She watched the Emperor slowly disappear in stages through the city, in and out of her view. She wouldn't trouble him with more dreams. But without her dream-connection with the Emperor, what would sustain her in her work? She walked back and forth at the foot of the south slope. After a while the youth fell into step beside her. She let herself be calmed by the rhythm of their walk.

As they approached his little house they slowed. How gracefully he had cut the supporting posts, how expertly positioned them. For the roof he had found a way to use overlapping leaves. Grasses were intertwined to make the walls, letting in a little light. How the light patterned the smoothed floor! In her studio she showed him her looms. At her gesture of invitation he sat before each loom in turn, trying each part and understanding how it worked. They sat until his silent presence became a pact.

The next day he swept away the old shimmering blue and green fragments as she tidied her space for the Emperor's autumn outfit. She had no idea what it would be like, but in the youth's company surely ideas would come to her as she wove. She took the time to enjoy this realization. As she threaded the loom swiftly and meticulously with a neutral warp, as she chose the individual strands of fine, sea-grey wool, as she wove the plain cloth with perfect evenness, she could feel his admiration. She set up a warp on a second loom for him to weave the less difficult part, the brightly patterned border.

In the youth's eagerness to learn and work he would never have left the studio. So she passed on invitations to him, invitations from her assistants that tempted her with company but would strain her silence. She walked with him once through the city so the townspeople would know who he was and greet him. At the palace the courtiers welcomed the diversion of an innocent face. He liked to listen to them, and be aware of the mysterious silence beyond their talk.

Thus the Minister kept some of her customary solitude. When the youth came back and told her everything he had seen, the familiar was made fresh by his telling. She was so eager to hear, it was all he could do to keep silent as they walked together carrying the Emperor's next three outfits through the dark city to the palace.Outfits which expressed the changing spirit in the studio, the colourful energy of autumn, the inwardness of winter, and the tenderness of spring.

The day after the spring ceremony the youth wandered at leisure toward the studio, contemplating possible futures for himself. He was called *Apprentice*. That had the ring of a title. He could become a Minister like her. He didn't mind silence. Or devote himself to her, take her away. Perhaps to the north side of the mountain. Did no one go there, even to explore? What did it mean, to be sacred?

As he wandered, he noticed the swindlers returning from the south, their donkeys laden with heavy chests. As they approached he hid behind a tree. Compared to the subtle colours in his Minister's studio, the colours the swindlers wore were screeching extremes. He could hear the discordant jangle of metal in their clothes as they passed him. Nevertheless, there was something splendid in their foreign style. He followed them discreetly to the palace.

The excited courtiers stirred the Minister of Innovation out of his long idleness. Before him, with grand gestures, the swindlers claimed they were now weavers. On their magic loom they could weave cloth that was invisible to fools. They proposed to create such cloth in full view and make it into a new outfit for the Emperor. The Minister of Innovation fell back asleep. But the titillated courtiers led the swindlers to the Minister of Adornment's old studio in the palace and helped unpack their trunks. Though the apprentice was suspicious of the strangely-shaped wooden parts, they did seem to fit together as a loom. The courtiers praised the warp as the swindlers were threading the loom. The apprentice recognized their gestures. They knew what they were doing. But he saw no thread at all, not in their trunks or anywhere around the studio.

The townspeople sensed something strange and came to the palace. The courtiers chipped peepholes for them in the outside walls of the studio and proudly described what the swindlers were weaving. The townspeople saw the loom but nothing on it. Could they be fools? If the Emperor wore clothes that were invisible to them, how could they fulfil their duty to behold him clothed? While some of them remained in mystified silence, others repeated with embellishments the courtiers' descriptions of the supposed, invisible cloth. Uneasiness spread through the city. The apprentice ran home to report to his Minister.

She amazed him by not being concerned at all. She immediately set up a third loom and a fourth and sent him back to the palace to watch and listen. Each new piece of information he brought back—how the invisible cloth was described by one person and then another, what discordant colours they claimed to see, whatever strange things were supposedly woven into it——the Minister incorporated harmoniously into the cloth on her looms. Even the metal bits, which she had directed him to beat thin and polish, set off the softness of the cloth.

On the eve of the summer ceremony the apprentice joined the townspeople outside the palace studio. The peepholes were larger now. Children, able to see into the studio, imitated the great last-minute fussing. The courtiers held up empty hangers, trying to disguise the lack of weight. They waved clothes-brushes in the air, while the swindlers appeared to pick off stray bits of thread. The courtiers themselves carried the invisible outfit toward the Imperial dressing chamber, out of sight of the crowd.

When the townspeople went home and everyone in the palace went to bed, the apprentice crept back to his Minister. Proud in her presence, he picked up the Emperor's real clothes. In spite of their elaborateness they were light. Remembering the metal bits he carefully kept the outfit quiet as he carried it through the dark city, his Minister beside him. Together in the Imperial dressing chamber they laid out the Emperor's clothes.

They crept home with their secret, crept the long way around the city, where no one would hear them giggling. Her sounds were precious to him. In the morning he encouraged her to rest at home, and tore himself away to the palace.

The Emperor appeared fully and magnificently clothed. The colours, sounding harsh when described in the palace studio, now blended. No one had mentioned headgear, but there it was, a natural extension of the clothes as they tapered upward. The bits of metal—even the courtiers had shuddered when they described them tinkled softly when the Emperor moved in certain ways. He started through the city toward the north slope of the mountain. Distractedly, but this did not perturb his Ministers or his bewildered courtiers, who flanked him.

The townspeople were astonished to see the Emperor clothed. Shame gripped them, shame that they had looked forward to seeing their neighbours appear as fools. In abashed silence they shook hands all around. Then in relief they swarmed around the swindlers and carried them high to the north slope, the apprentice in their midst.

41

The swindlers, too, were astonished. It was all they could do to hold on. The apprentice, enjoying their consternation, stayed near them and followed them back to the palace studio. How had this happened, the swindlers demanded of each other. Had the clothes become visible overnight? Surely these clothes resembled all the conflicting descriptions they had dispersed. There had been foul play, more foul than theirs. They agreed not to give up, for they still believed that along with their bad name went their mission to expose the Emperor. Besides, they had encouraged bets among the courtiers and a few of the townspeople about what the Emperor was hiding under his clothes. They had stood to gain a great deal of money, which they had planned to spend when they went south again. And so they worked more slowly on the supposed new autumn outfit, playing for time, encouraging more betting, and trying to figure out how their plans had been foiled. They worked, they delayed, right through the autumn.

Though the ceremony was delayed, the seasons progressed and passed. To the autumn-coloured threads on her loom, the Minister of Adornment added the traditional white of winter. When the apprentice returned from the palace and reported that the Emperor's supposed new outfit would be less elaborate than the first, she removed the more colourful threads from her work and laid them aside. When he reported that the swindlers seemed to be accomplishing very little, she slowed down. She showed him the fine points of how she adjusted the design. Then he picked up the colourful threads and wove them on one of the other looms, designing as he went along. A ribboned garment for his Minister, then one for himself.

Without processions to mark the seasons, the citizens lost track. Whenever the time felt right, the Ministers came out of the palace and went about their work, the townspeople joining in as they wished. The apprentice and his Minister strolled by in their colourful clothes.

The Minister of Roads, tamping down the streets with his assistants, stopped with one correctly-angled foot in the air when he saw them. The Minister of Air Traffic and her assistants looked down, and the stars disappeared from their eyes. The Minister of Commerce and his assistants let the new currency swirl and escape into the air. A pure hum drew the two of them to the Minister of Eloquence and his assistants, who were listening to the amaryllis trumpets in the palace garden. Leaving the flowers to darken with held breath, the Minister of Eloquence stepped in front of the

Minister of Adornment and looked directly into her face. Forced to remember her position, she abruptly turned back toward the studio. In her wake the apprentice's ribbons swirled around him and rested across his eyes.

He could hardly keep up with her determined strides. By the time he reached the studio she had already changed back to her everyday clothes and was at her loom, looking for a detail of her weaving to pay attention to. He was hurt. He had done nothing wrong. With the luxury of time he would have protested. But, still in his colourful clothes, he was thrown right back into his work. For the swindlers had decided their second outfit was nearly ready. Their fussing, and the courtiers', this time attracted a larger though less apprehensive crowd. When the supposed outfit had been taken to the dressing chamber, the apprentice returned to the mountain studio. Then he crept back across the city by himself carrying the Emperor's real clothes. At least she trusted him that much.

In the morning, from the porch of the studio, he watched the Emperor come into view. The new outfit, white, with hints of spring colours in the inner garments, still managed to suggest the sea. As the procession came closer he could see the courtiers' and townspeople's still bewildered relief. How had the clothes become visible? They kept wondering right through the ceremony. No sooner had the procession turned back toward the city than his Minister prepared her loom for the next outfit.

When the apprentice entered the studio to report what was happening in the palace, she barely broke the rhythm of her work to listen. The cloth on her loom had progressed faster than he would have thought possible, and she seemed to know without his saying that the Emperor's next clothes would be simpler still. He was proud of her. He was petulant. How did she always know what was just right? How could she produce such wonders and ignore him?


The swindlers, supposedly at work on their third outfit, became lazy, the apprentice reported. Weaving was hard work, with or without thread. They brought their park benches into the palace studio and slept on them any time of night or day. They quarrelled openly. Whose stupid idea had it been? How would they get out of this trap they had made? They threatened to hang each other, if only they had the means to make rope.

At first the courtiers enjoyed listening, for quarrels were rare.

But when the swindlers slept, the coutiers began to think and realized they had been duped. They had risked putting their Emperor in a bad light. In the night they ran the swindlers out of the city as discreetly as they could, though they couldn't prevent the braying of the donkeys.

The Emperor appeared the next morning fully clothed, and the courtiers and townspeople realized who had been their protectors. When the ancient names had been intoned and history contemplated once again, the Minister of Eloquence set up his hum in the air. He announced that since the Emperor's penchant for clothes had given rise to a hoax that endangered the self-respect of his citizens, the Emperor would henceforth be content with the clothes he already had. The Minister of Adornment could retire. Since she already possessed the highest honour by virtue of her position, and since the apprentice had the courage to recognize the empty loom for what it was, he was declared a hero, the first hero ever in the seaside dynasty.

The apprentice thought, *Surely this is the first step. The Minister of Loyalty, he could be called. Or the Invited One, Minister of Sociability. The Minister of Applause and Handshakes!* All he desired was to stay and enjoy his glory, expressed in the colourful clothes he had been wearing all along, as if in readiness.

Now that he was a hero and had become an attractive young man, among his many invitations were the kind that women make. He accepted every one. As he passed the studio he would see his old Minister unmoving at her loom, looking out over the city. When he returned he would stop by and report everything he had done. Sometimes, happier than he could bear, he would come into the studio and sit quietly. Or weave for himself, and reflect. He was young. He liked to climb. He liked to shout. He wanted to experience real weather. He was a hero. He could fight. He could win. He could make the clothes to make himself whatever he wanted to be.

One outfit after another he wove, each more colourful than the last. He packed them in bundles, which he balanced on his back. Dazzling with purpose, ribbons streaming behind him as he faced the wind, he picked out a zigzag path up the north slope of Historical Mountain.

From her window she caught glimpses of him as he neared the west slope. At each turn he planted a coloured banner before he veered back eastward. She watched until there was a progression of banners brightly visible through the trees, then against the snow toward the peak. She turned and went out to her porch. Through the city she saw townspeople, courtiers among them, carrying packs toward the mountain to join him. Of course, she thought, it was the privilege of youth to repeat.

She covered her windows with old samples. What was she now? She sat on the floor among her looms. Eyes closed, curled in on herself, she waited to know what was really important to her. She found herself remembering over and over the mountain above her, the city roads bordered by flowers, the intricate city itself spreading down to the sea. She remembered her assistants, their silent comfort, and she missed them.


The Emperor no longer led processions to the mountain. Instead, he wandered as he pleased, with anyone joining him who wished. He wore his clothes carelessly fastened, his headgear askew, his masks loose. Then he wore fewer and fewer clothes, until it was obvious he had no visible body. The Minister of Eloquence cleared his throat as a summons, and announced that the Silent Emperor, His Embodiment of Adornment, would henceforth remove the word *Embodiment* from his title. Thus freed, when the Emperor got tired of clothes he went about unencumbered. It was similarly announced, among the lilies of the field, that the Emperor would give up the word *Adornment*. He usually wore something on his head, though, for he was fond of the ingenious headgear she had made him. And he wanted the citizens to know where he was and not bump into him. Or would they walk right through him, he wondered?

What happened was that more of them walked away. These were the rest of the courtiers and those of the townspeople who respected an Emperor who looked the part. Body or no body, he could at least have remained dressed. Sorry to see an end to the regular spectacle of processions, they, too, followed the bright path up the mountain, taking their children by the hand.

The Emperor's favourite place to wander was the beach. Not bothering with an announcement, he dropped the word *Silent* and

45

was left with no title at all. Long-forgotten sounds came from his throat. They came out in a playful, rhythmic chant that blended with the sound of the sea. The Ministers played at each other's work on their roundabout way to the beach to gather near him.

Streaming in the other direction were still more townspeople, muttering about an Emperor who changed his ways. They hadn't minded that he never spoke. But they would not stay and be embarrassed by the nonsense that now came out of his supposed mouth. As they approached the mountain, their children ran ahead, encouraged by the sound of lively music and banners bright against the snowy peak.


From her studio she heard them pass, the last of her former purpose passing with them. Now she was drawn to the beach. She dismantled her oldest loom. It, too, had done its work. She gathered up some of the parts and a few scraps of cloth to take along. Thinking of her Emperor, his perfection, his imperfections, aware there were aspects of him she didn't know, she walked through the deserted city.

On the beach the Ministers, also laden, were rambling after an Imperial headdress as if searching for an appropriate spot. When they seemed to have found it, they stopped. The headdress, the old fiery one with the red now faded, was gently laid on the sand. Around it in a pattern the Ministers placed what they had brought, paving tools, currency, flowers, bits of fallen stars. In the space they left for her she placed her own offerings.

They all turned toward the sea. Some of her assistants were there, those she liked best, her own age. One took her hand. The Emperor took the other! She could feel it! They all joined hands as if to close the ring, a ring around the sea. There weren't enough of them, but that didn't matter. Having one common sound, they did not speak. They faded till they could barely see each other. They stood there, swinging their arms, jostling, laughing, embracing as best they could the changing colours of the sea.

46

# II

# The Fox, The Grapes, And The Author

In this story the fox gets the grapes. You may have caught the incident on the news. Just as the prize-winning vineyard was being shown, a small red fox trotted right in front of the TV cameras, snapped off a cluster of grapes, and, as a parting gesture, flicked its tail against the fencepost.

My fencepost.

My vineyard.

My former vineyard.

Here I am on the subway with nowhere to go, riding back and forth to get some perspective on what happened. Lulled by the train, I recall the sunlit vines I worked among for innocent pleasure. A lurch of the train brings back that fateful rainy season when, unable to work, I took refuge in the library. There, as I browsed, I chanced upon the ancient fable, the vine that had grown up a tree, the grapes high out of reach, the fox that told itself the grapes were sour anyway, and the moral, that it is easy to disparage what we can't have.

The fable possessed me. Producing sweeter and sweeter grapes, I worked with a firm sense of *noblesse oblige* as I imagined some poor fox looking on, ready to turn tail with its pitiable sour-grapes attitude. Intrigued by a creature so different from myself, I went back to the library. I found that in preference to grapes foxes eat insects, amphibians, reptiles, rodents, and, when these are not readily available, domestic fowl. How much grander was the fable to me now, its grapes symbolizing something mysterious, as do apples or figs! How much more glorious was the task I had taken on, perpetuating this venerable fable, this ultimate story! Yet here I am, possessed also by this other story that is emerging in spite of me on the subway, spilling out so urgently that I can barely write it down in the margins of found newspaper. The story of my ruin.

In my vineyard, as was customary, the vines were trained to

49

a modest height which implied that foxes long ago had learned their place. Prize or no prize, my vineyard was really not much different from anyone else's. Except that mine was where the pivotal incident took place. A fox, undaunted by its ancestral reputation, took a chance at some grapes. Just as one of the TV cameras was panning past this year's blue ribbon and along a row of vines, a small red fox trotted in, made a little jump, and snapped off a particularly luscious-looking cluster.

At this point you may wonder how the grapes actually tasted. Humiliated as I am, I would gladly stop and speculate awhile. Perhaps that would foil the inexorable chain of events and I could go home. But no, the story doesn't even pause to consider the taste of the grapes. It seems to have a more insidious purpose.

As the grapes touched the fox's lips, thousands of years of frustration surged through its heart. Vengefully aware of its position *vis à vis* the cameras, it flicked its red, red tail against a fencepost until sparks flew and the dry wood kindled. A quick last frame of the fox disappearing with the grapes, untasted, dangling from a stem between its teeth. Then the commercial. So you wouldn't have seen the flames take hold or the vineyard burn to the ground, vines, trellises, even the shed where I stored my tools and slept.

I count my losses:

My vineyard, of course.

My grandiose illusions, for, possessed as I was by the ancient fable, I fancied myself its hero.

And the fable itself, now spoiled for practical purposes: now that the fox has the grapes, what will become of the moral? What of the sour-grapes attitude, potentially useful, I realize now. Will it simply die out and leave us to face our failures unconsoled?

A wealth of psychological questions comes to mind. But the library is closed for the night. Here I am on the subway, travelling back and forth with nowhere to go.

You may fear that in my homelessness I covet someone else's vineyard. No danger of that. Vineyards demand hard labour. Vineyards are prime targets for arson. And grapes aren't what they used to be, anyway.

50

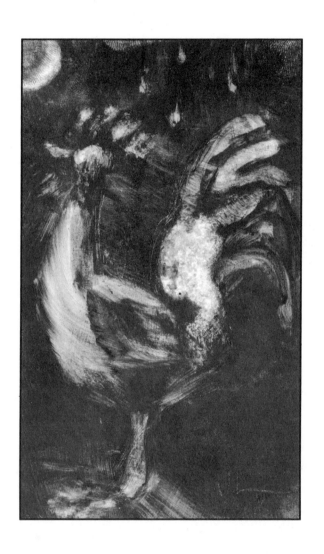

# Chicken Little, The Prophet

He found the other chickens strange. In the presence of a rainbow they would merely glance up and then go back to pecking at the ground.

For himself, the gentle miracles of the sky were all the sustenance he wanted, the play of puffy clouds, warm showers that barely dampened his thin feathers, breezes so slight he had to keep extra still to catch their fragrance. Though the sky itself worried him, young as he was. At first, when he had broken through his shell to see what was up there, the pristine blue lay flat over the plain from horizon to horizon. Now it was often slightly askew in one direction or another. What could Chicken Little do but observe its daily changes?

The elders thought there was something wrong with his neck, for he was always looking the other way. They picked out bits of corn and grit for him, poor thing. They were fond of him as they were of the chick who was always gazing into the stream and swaying, and the one who was transfixed by trees and kept bumping up against them. They knew that eventually even the strangest chicks succumbed to the call of the flesh and adopted regular habits. At dusk they nudged him toward the roosting tree.

Chicken Little gladly put his fears aside and nestled in among the warm breath and feathers. For there in the long, mild evenings the elders kept alive their chicken lore and passed it into the waiting minds of the chicks. They told of mysterious creatures, part dreamed and part believed. Legendary ancestors, the small, exotic fowl that lived in the jungle, whatever that was. Faraway cousins whose tails fanned out and were full of green-gold coins. Dangerous, masked creatures that stole eggs, and others, red-furred and crafty, that lured lone chickens into their dens for unmentioned purposes. Featherless, two-legged creatures that built squared shelters taller than roosting trees—who knew what else such beings could do? There were laws against all these creatures, but the chickens shuddered nevertheless. To calm themselves for sleep they

53

told of the Chicken King, off in his royal tree, who made such laws to keep them safe. Laws also against fighting, quarrelling, mockery, confrontation, anything that might disturb the chickens' peace of mind. Thunderstorms, for example, which nearly scared the chickens out of their tree not long ago.

Chicken Little could never get his fill of such talk. He felt, he dared to feel, it was all connected to him, and he to the glittering sky. In the sweet security of the roosting tree he tried to stay awake by counting stars.

Sometimes the stars seemed to jar. At first he thought it was just himself jarring himself awake. But once at dawn, as the King crowed in the distance, the sky slipped and remained at a precarious angle. Thin cracks spread over it. And Chicken Little knew the sky was falling.

For all the thrill of frightening themselves with tree-talk the chickens had never experienced real danger. Suddenly Chicken Little's voice, wild with impending disaster, assailed them. *The sky is falling!* he blurted at a nearby chick. She hushed him and stepped in among her companions. He came near and tried again. These were his tree-mates. *The sky is falling and the chickens will fall soon after!* They exposed their bony backs to him. What had happened to their old Chicken Little, who would gently sidle up to them, his gaze fixed in the opposite direction? He tried the hens, all mothers to him. *The sky is falling and the chickens will fall soon after! Come to the horizon and be saved!* The hens squawked as loud as they could so as not to hear him.

He dared approach a group of roosters. He was scrawny, he had lost most of his down, his real feathers were a long time growing in. Would the roosters, suave and sure, listen to him?

*The sky is falling!* The roosters stepped deliberately from one foot to the other. *The sky is falling and the chickens will fall soon after. We will lose the freedom of the plain. We will be confined and slaughtered. The very name "chicken" will be debased. Come to the horizon and be saved!* The roosters stepped faster and faster and flexed their necks.

Law or no law, Chicken Little ran for his life. He ran, hopping and flapping, until the sky shuddered and stopped him short. The sky had greyed. Against this background stood the royal tree. Yes, he would tell the King.

Bemused and ready to be entertained, the huge old King perched at the top of the tree. His green tailfeathers arched over the fluffy-feathered queens of every colour and pattern. Chicken Little

54

mustered what dignity he could and called up, *The sky is falling!*

The King took up the challenge. *Surely the sky falls every day. What are rain, snow, and sunshine, if not aspects of the sky? Even the stars long to fall on our illustrious flock, though few succeed.*

Chicken Little's eyes were urgent with tears. *The sky is falling, and the chickens will fall soon after. Kings will be forgotten. Equality will prevail. The chickens will be more comfortable, more important, less glorious, less free. Come to the horizon and be saved!*

A whoosh of wing-feathers applauded him. The King, however, had felt the shiver of truth. *Who dares confront the court with prophecy?* He glared down, considering punishment. But Chicken Little was oblivious to the danger. He had just discovered what he was. A prophet.

A hard drizzle started. The queens drew closer to the King and avoided catching Chicken Little's eye. No room in the tree for a prophet. He huddled bitterly in a small bush. Above the rain the sky buckled. His impulse was to run and save himself, but what was a chicken without his flock? And what was his flock, that disdained their own chick who was trying to save them? When the rain stopped he strayed in the direction of the horizon, wandering in fearful circles and getting thinner. But as he watched the darkening, slowly-heaving sky his fear gave way to pride. He was a prophet! Hard-hearted with frustration, now he wanted the pleasure of being right. *Left, right, left, right, sky, falling, sky, falling,* he called out, testing his prophecy, as he marched straight to the horizon and beyond. And at last, as if waiting for this signal, the sky fell.

It fell over many days and many nights. Grey porridges of cloud splatted, far-reaching, onto the plain. Gelatinous chunks of bright light blue wobbled into place. Sinuous wisps of cloud alighted here and there. In the hushed spaces of darkness sharp stars were suspended. Splits of lightning set the plain trembling. In the earth-bound thunder, mountains rose near the quaking plain. The force of the fall catapulted Chicken Little up to where the sky had been.

Beak over claw he tumbled through a haze of indefinite twilight, stopping, dizzy and vindicated, over the centre of the plain. He felt neither wind nor calm, but an undercurrent of agitation. The tiny would-be drops of rain or flakes of snow spiralled slowly around him. To steady himself he looked down and focused on the pieces of sky, some scattered, some piled on each other, as they had fallen onto the plain. Little whirlwinds grew strong and carved into the plain, turning streams into rivers, seas into oceans. Propelled noisily over the waters, strange shelters approached, carrying the featherless, two-legged creatures the chickens had not quite believed in.

Chicken Little watched these creatures with their ominous inventions settle on the plain and he chuckled. He was safe, suspended in the exquisite cold that preserved his young flesh. And he was about to enjoy seeing the fall of the surviving chickens, who disdained him.


From the sheltered spaces between the first-fallen pieces of sky, the chickens ventured out into an unfamiliar haze bounded by mountains. They soon accepted their new surroundings. They admired the featherless creatures—humans, they called themselves cleverly digging into the plain with tools. When they failed to hear their king crow they took this honour upon themselves. Happy to be scratching in the dust once more, they celebrated with a joke.

*Where's Chicken Little?* one asked.

*Up in the sky,* another answered.

*...falling...falling,* a third mocked in falsetto. And the chickens laughed. They knew the sky wasn't up there any more. They laughed with their heads high and their yellow beaks open wide.

Some chickens felt the joke was in poor taste and objected to its use. Even though the pieces of the old sky on the plain were beginning to dissipate, even though traces of a new sky were forming above, the fall had occurred, just as Chicken Little had prophesied. The unfulfilled, second half of his prophecy, that the chickens would fall soon after, might be triggered by anything untoward, such as an irreverent joke. But the jokesters would not be dissuaded, and there were many of them. As an aid to quarrelling they formed political parties, The Party for Using the Joke to Forget the Second Half of the Prophecy, and The Party for Using the Joke to Defy the Second Half of the Prophecy. Neither party knew what it meant, that chickens would fall—chickens now spent most of their time on the ground anyway—but they were prepared to fight to the death, so long as they could silence the doomsayers with their shrieks.

A fortuitous solution came from the humans, who were looking for diversion. They invited the chickens to live among them and fight. The chickens did their best. In this new, apparently

56

lawless, age they gratefully entrusted their safety to human kindness. When the humans tired of bloodshed, the chickens offered up their flesh and even their eggs so as not to be forgotten. The humans developed the habit of using chickens and eggs for food. When the humans enclosed their barnyards with modern fences just for them, the chickens felt secure among their benefactors. Though some jealous humans referred to them in a derogatory way, chickens became the proudest and most numerous fowl in the world.

Protected by human technology, the chickens lost their fear of thunderstorms. Indeed, the regular storms seemed to relieve the new sky and keep it safely in place. But in the leisure of having their food so plentifully provided by the humans, the memory of the unfulfilled half of Chicken Little's prophecy gnawed at their peace of mind as a sore tooth would gnaw at a human. The elders, who were chicks when he was going on about the sky, blamed Chicken Little. They blamed him when the weather changed too frequently, when it didn't change frequently enough, and when it became a tiresome subject.

Whatever they said, Chicken Little liked being mentioned so often, more often than the King had ever been. He couldn't strut in the sky, for fear of falling through, so he did one better. He slid back and forth, his speed keeping him safely on the cold blue surface. He lorded over the Star creatures, threatening the Scorpion with his beak and taunting the Little Bear tethered to the Pole. He played with rainbows. Up here they were circular, and he liked to pose at their centre. If only the chickens below could see him now!

The elder chickens dreamed that they slipped and slid with nothing under their feet while Chicken Little looked on coolly. They hoped the chicks hadn't shared this dream. They didn't want any awkward questions. But no, there were the chicks in the barnyard, happily feasting.

Their own chicks, every bit as glib and well-mannered as humans! How far they had come from days of the sky-soiled plain! The elders grew nostalgic for the old chicken lore and longed to pass it on. They wanted the chicks to be proud of their roots as well as their present, privileged position. But how to teach them? The system of tree-time talks had broken down. Now, in barns, the chickens spent their nights thriving on human music.

The solution came once again from the humans. Bored with education as they knew it, they fancied grass-roots knowledge. In the leisure of having their food so plentifully provided by the chickens, they became curious about what the chickens knew. The beaming chicken elders remembered what they could, and the humans wrote down what they thought they heard. This was called history and taught to the children. The chicks overheard the children at play.

When the chicks repeated what they had learned, the elders were confused. They reflected, they deliberated, they denied, but the insidious bias was clear. The humans were mocking them. Though the humans invited them to share their traffic lights, the lights changed too fast for any chicken to cross the road. The humans disputed which had come first, *the* chicken or *the* egg, whereas chickens clearly came from eggs and eggs from chickens and there were plenty of both. They featured chickens in brightly-coloured magazines, but more often than not they called them poultry and showed them cooked.

The humans considered the story of Chicken Little a mere fanciful tale and distorted it. They introduced extraneous fowl, a duck, a goose, a turkey. They implied that Chicken Little had gone to a human king, as if they could imagine no other. According to them, not only had Chicken Little been wrong, but he had been defeated by a fox, a creature never mentioned by name in real chicken lore. Out of pride the elders were forced to set the record straight. Gathering the chicks together away from the food, they started the story from the beginning and told some of the truth. They admitted that, when the sky was falling, something that looked like Chicken Little had been seen at the horizon tumbling upward.

To the chicks this tale was a revelation. In the context of human tales Chicken Little was their hero, his dignity at odds with the tone of voice the chicken elders used when they referred to him, the same tone of voice the humans used when they referred to chickens in general. Educated, uncorrupted, and as yet unfearful, the chicks were inspired by Chicken Little. They became watchers of the skies.

They stood under trees and looked up, hoping to find something they could report to the King. (Of course the chickens no longer had a king, but the expression *going to tell the King* lent importance to any journey.) They saw injustice in the stars. Though human civilization was unthinkable without the support of chickens, the chickens were not represented among the constellations, which the humans named.

The elders recognized the truth in this and tentatively came round. Under the circumstances the idea of a chicken hero, even Chicken Little, appealed to them. They thought it was cute when the chicks prepared to join him and redress the wrong. One chicken in the sky did not a constellation make. The chicks trekked to the mountains, to the highest, most barren places, where they fasted and were silent.

Chicken Little sobered at the sight of the chicks, so close now, coming to him to be saved. What would he teach them? His own supremacy, of course. And everything else he knew. Though limited in practical value it would develop their minds in ways undreamed of by the common flock. How to appraise an unstable sky. How to recognize a prophecy. How to be heard—he must have learned something from his failure. To be gracious, however capriciously portrayed by history. That chickens were right and good, and beautiful in their way as were the stars.


With the chicks so long in the mountains the elders became uneasy. No real harm had come from the brood that ate only flowers, nor from the brood that wore their tailfeathers well away from what tailfeathers were supposed to protect. But when these chicks climbed high and stayed there, getting so thin that a gust of wind could actually sweep them into the sky, the elders feared that whatever was up there might be reminded of the unfulfilled second half of the prophecy, whatever it meant.

To prevent this from happening and, of course, protect the chicks, they created a specialized occupation, which, in the human tradition, they referred to as one of the helping professions. Up to the tops of the mountains climbed the elders, bearing acorns, apples, pumpkins, and bits of garbage they had salvaged with permission from the humans. All these they would use as ammunition.

As the first chick was struck, with his budding comb and still-flexible breastbone, Chicken Little's flesh-memory wrenched awake. Young voices were crying out his name. He reached down with his wing, and his arrested feathers prickled to grow again. Oh, to be near those chicks! To be near any chickens, even their tormentors! Surely the worst sighed sometimes in their sleep. To stand on the plain once more, to eat, to roost among the whispering of hens to their chicks! To be among his kind, even in markets, from which they never returned! Prophet that he was, subject of a tale, he was still flesh. He had been right and the others wrong, but surely

59

to be so lonely was the greater wrong?

Perhaps he could still grow! He would go back and save them all! He tried to jump down through the sky but the relentless blue bounced him back. Feeling exposed in the sun, he curled in on himself. He tried to rock toward the edge, to fall over the horizon, but he kept rolling back in circles like an egg. He curled in tighter and began to spin. Jostled by clouds, lifted by wind, sped on by the fevers of hope and despair, faster and faster he spun until he crashed among the cold, cold stars.


Goading the chicks down the mountains, the elders shouted slogans at them. *Fearful and flavourful, these are the bywords. To be fed and to feed is the truth of all flesh.* They continued to pelt them, and there was always the combined din of victorious and sorrowful squawking. And so, when the tiny *ping* that marked the end of Chicken Little tingled in the sky, no one heard it.

But a slow easing of urgency, a flooding of peace, spread wide over the plain, as if the prophecy had never been, nor history, nor tree-times. Among their human benefactors the remaining chickens lived happily for a while, and their kind prevailed.

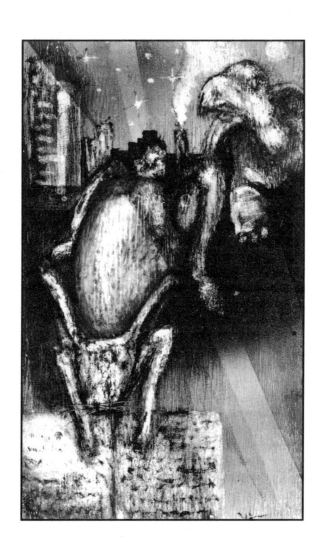

# The Hare, The Tortoise, And The Human Race

The hare was...hare-brained.

The tortoise congratulated itself on inventing so apt an adjective and added it to the dictionary. The tortoise might have described itself as taciturn, or tenacious, or turgid, but no one in the whole of the kingdom understood such words. Not even humans, it thought with a mixture of pride and exasperation.

The tortoise liked to shape words in its silent mouth. Words from the soft-cornered dictionary it carried in the folds of skin near its heart. The tortoise had slept the nights of its youth with this same dictionary pressing into the soft flesh of its back. With body flat and limbs extended it had slept, as its shell grew large enough to accommodate both body and book in comfort. This memory kept the tortoise strong through adverse times.

Humans coveted the hare for its fur and its lucky feet. If they bothered at all about the tortoise, they thought of the soup it might become. The tortoise balked at being seen in such a limited light. It was one of Aesop's creatures. It believed it had been created to teach humans, and resolved to make them as pedantic as itself.

The dictionary was a good beginning, but the tortoise knew it would need more books, as well. It made its way laboriously through the kingdom, from forest to field to as far into the city as it could stomach, interpreting what it saw and writing down everything it thought the humans needed to understand. Back in the forest it checked over its work. Drawn by its silent concentration, other forest creatures crept near. It took this opportunity to describe them, too. It filed its papers cleverly among its folds. Then scattering the forest creatures with one look of its steady, speckled eye, the tortoise resumed its circuit.

Relentless as it was in preparing to teach the humans, the tortoise doubted they would ever be ready to learn. Instead, the whole human race followed the hare's fast-changing antics. Round and round the city hopped the hare, filling its insatiable ears with cacophony. Motorcycles, airplanes, construction, radio and TV at the same time—the accumulating noises clung to the hare like an aura, louder and louder, and the humans cheered it on.

The tortoise tried not to question why Aesop had created the hare. From time to time the hare returned to the forest to relax in the quiet of home. But its accompanying noises never died out completely, and even the faintest noise tormented the tortoise. The tortoise spared no effort in turning its back on the hare. It lumbered the other way in search of a peaceful spot.

But the hare goaded the tortoise, who annoyed it by moving so slowly. It hopped zigzags over the tortoise's shell. The tortoise looked neither right nor left but continued on its way. *Tough tortoise! Tough tortoise!* chattered the hare, thumping a little dance to the rhythm. Then it hopped in front of the tortoise and fell asleep directly in its path.

*Hyper! Hare-brained!* grunted the tortoise. *Hooligan! Hasenpfeffer!*

The tortoise's competitive urge bulged in its neck. The more the humans admired the hare, the more disgusting and the more urgent the idea of rivalry became to the tortoise. It feared it might waste itself trapped in conflict with the hare and fail in its lofty mission. But generally it practised the rueful discipline it had set up for itself: to contemplate the hare without rage. It escaped into its own private conflict, whether to retreat into its shell and sulk, or into its dictionary and deliberate.

The hare, in the vanguard of human fashion, hopped back to the city with its fur washed, oiled, powdered, permed, moussed. It shaved itself once and some humans mistook it for a long-eared slug. The tortoise was quick to chuckle at the hare's embarrassment. But when its fur grew back the hare learned to change colours simply by the force of will. Bright colours, clear colours—the tortoise was just thinking it might some day admire the hare's ingenuity, when the hare, pulsing in a multicoloured pattern, caught the fancy of the human king.

This was the hare's undoing. Summoned to the palace, it was an object of endless wonder. Even when it tried to relax back to its natural colour for the night, it sometimes hiccupped, and its colours flashed out all at once and lit up the sky. Ordered to hiccup again and again, the hare soon expired in full spectrum.

Forthwith its fur was claimed and its memory sanctified.

The king draped himself in its fur, with colours and lucky feet showing to good advantage. In time the king took on the hare's personality, and other humans followed in emulation. Careless of etymology, they used the word *hairy* to describe their new pace of life.

The tortoise, forced by integrity, added this new meaning to the dictionary. As it did so, it considered scratching out any words that might apply to itself, and leaving the dictionary by the side of the road for the untaught humans to use at their peril. But, mindful of its mission, it hid the dictionary far back in its shell and retreated through the forest to a small crack in the barren cliffs. There it prepared to bide its time through a succession of kings and human values until the humans were ready to be taught.

But it dreamed of the hare and woke shuddering. To calm itself it scanned the dictionary for a companion. With triceratops gone, perhaps a toad? A tarantula? The thought of support was enough to strengthen the tortoise's sense of mission. There was no end to what the humans needed to understand. And so the tortoise walked once more from forest to field and, with a grunt, into the city as well, gratified to find a few more useful details to interpret and write down.

By this time the tortoise's body had shrunk with age, and its shell was well able to accommodate the proliferating papers. When the papers shifted and made its flesh itch, it spread them out, reread them with satisfaction, and bound them into books, which it tucked away here and there on its person. Thus prepared, but despairing that its mission might never be fulfilled, the tortoise walked more slowly. Some days it didn't bother to walk at all.

One morning the tortoise woke up with the impression of being in two places. It could smell itself simmering in a cauldron. At the same time, there it was intact with its books, translucent, transcending the soup, rising to heaven.

On the throne sat Aesop with a rainbow over his head. Aesop was beckoning. The tortoise lumbered up to what it hoped was its rightful resting place. It laid its life's worth of books under the throne. Then standing back, gazing up at Aesop for some sign of acceptance, the tortoise was alerted by a familiar whizzing sound. It froze in suspicion. What it had taken for a rainbow turned out to be the path of the rarefied hare hopping back and forth so fast its colours blurred into stripes. From the kingdom below, the tortoise heard faint sounds from the city. The humans, still attuned to the hare, had built amusement parks in rainbow colours.

Without its ballast of books the tortoise trembled. But Aesop stroked its head and calmed his beloved creature. He explained that in heaven we are free to lay aside our differences and become what we once despised. The tortoise took a long time to integrate this piece of wisdom. To become what we once despised.

Well, a tortoise didn't question its creator. It relaxed its habitual frown and invited its cousin the hare to rest. Tortoise and hare sat down together. The tortoise allowed the hare to paint its shell in subtle colours. For the newly-discovered pleasure of showing off, it danced a little.

With the hare subdued, the human pace slowed down. There was a trend below to move to the country. When the hare became bored the humans did, too. Though the hare was aware of the humans waiting for guidance, it had no more taste for its old ways. Disoriented, it hopped listlessly this way and that.

Seeing its cousin in this new, heavenly light, the tortoise was moved to write about the hare. It settled beside the throne, opened one of its books, and described the historical, harlequin hare; the harmonious, humble hare; the hare heart-rending in its present state.

With the book still open before it, the tortoise stopped to reflect. What could it do to help the hare? It was heartened to see the hare, now curious and purposeful, hop toward the throne. Then the tortoise remembered its mission and rejoiced. For the hare looked into the tortoise's book and began to read. And the tortoise knew it had won the human race.

# The Possible Cheese

A farmer came out of his dell to look for a wife. It was his turn in the old traditional song, and he needed a wife to dance through its motions with him. Of course he would adapt the song to fit the times. He stood on the hill and looked around.

Along the path came a woman, singing and carrying baskets. When the farmer saw she was strong, his fervour rose. He described their future: they would have a child, a dog, a cat, a mouse (he couldn't help that), and a cheese, a magnificent cheese that would stand alone among cheeses. At his words her eyes brimmed with like-mindedness. She, too, was of the times. To plight their troth they made a cheese together.

There wasn't enough milk on the farm in the dell for such a cheese so they collected some from the neighbours. As they walked down the hill with the heavy pails, as they cut the curd, tied it up to drain, and pressed it into the huge, specially-made form, they talked over their intentions for their cheese. It would have dignity, to stand alone while everyone else in the song got to choose a companion. It would be noble, a substance to be honoured and obeyed. For, walking on the wooded hill in the moonlight, they confided their belief that cheese pre-dated people. Cheese was wiser than us all. As the luminous moon was set off by the dark sky, they would display their dark-waxed cheese in a brightly lit gazebo they would build for it. Or softly lit, if that would be more effective. When it was time, when the cheese was wrapped in cloth and freshly dipped in wax, they went off to get married. They came right back and used their new rings to stamp a pattern around the rim of the cheese.

Now married, they argued. Where to build the gazebo? To display their valuable cheese on the hill and attract viewers or protect it in the dell? They argued daily, sometimes changing sides, but arguing nevertheless. They stopped only to turn the cheese with proper reverence. They made smaller cheeses, which they sold to the neighbours. The neighbours were curious about the rumoured big

69

cheese, but when they saw the door of the maturing-room shut they scoffed that there was none. The neighbours knew, as did the farmer and his wife, that until the cheese was shown in a proper setting, until it had been seen and admired, it was merely a possible cheese. Ripe, perhaps, but merely possible, like an awaited prince or a reclusive billionaire. The farmer and his wife argued about this, too. Which did their possible cheese more resemble? They argued until they slept.

They dreamed of blind mice trembling under the threat of a knife. Three mice—there was so much foolishness in the world it took three mice not to see it. The farmer and his wife didn't talk about their dream. Loyal to their cheese, they argued about the gazebo. Should they use screen or glass?

They dreamed of a cat that spent nine lives stuck in a bag. When they woke they remembered its awful noises. But they didn't talk about their dream. They turned to important matters. Would a refrigerated gazebo ruin the cheese or add to their prestige with its newfangledness?

They dreamed of a dog begging to forget it had ever been wild. It barked at bare cupboards, then dug over and over into the ground with nothing to bury. They didn't talk about their dream. But in order to stop such dreams they agreed on something. They would build a bigger house, the better to entertain the future admirers of their cheese.

Days and nights they stayed awake cutting wood on the hill and carrying it down to the farm in the dell. When at last they rested, wood on the ground beside them, they fell fast asleep. They dreamed their cheese heaved itself off its table and rolled around the phantom gazebo. It rolled through the dell up to the top of the hill, back down and through the dell up to the top of the hill on the moon side—so beautiful for that instant, who could tell which was the reflection of the other?—back down and through the dell, increasing speed, up and over the first hill and down the other side toward the river. Mouse, cat, and dog ran frenzied after each other after the cheese. There might have been young laughter but the farmer and his wife didn't stop to think of that. They ran toward the river to save their cheese. They ran until they woke, and remembered it was safe at home.

There in the maturing-room they slowed to the silent atmosphere their cheese commanded. They got accustomed to its human smell, its dark wax glistening with sweat, as they were. In this long moment, milder than a sleep-dream, they regained their senses and were still.

The only moving thing was the furtive mouse on the other side of the cheese. They knew there was a mouse in the song but were nonplussed to find it here in their well-kept house. But it was sweetly small. They watched its alert movements as it dug into the cheese and nibbled. Well-meaning, they came closer, but the mouse was shy and ran away. Reverently they walked around the cheese to the hole the mouse had left. From the sides of the hole they broke off pungent pieces, tasted them, and ate them.

Outdoors they stood in the light of the moon. The mouse tried to hide among their feet, then squeaked and shot across the field with the cat after it. The dog woke from its hungry sleep and followed. The farmer and his wife ran too, joining in the furry vigour, till their laughter felled them to the ground. And into the beating space between their hearts came the waiting child.

And so they danced through the old traditional song. The cut wood sprouted where it lay and grew back into the hill. The neighbours came to witness and to sing. The song re-echoed through the dell, once more survived the times, and kept us circling.

# The Sprats' Spat

She ate the fat, and he, the lean. That's how it was. Until the neighbours who kept one eye on the TV began to watch the Sprats with the other.

Jack built the house with saw and hammer and stayed lean. His wife baked or nibbled or lounged around staying fat. She dreamed about him working up there on the roof. Sometimes she went out and handed him nails. That's how it used to be. She loved and he worked, it seemed to the neighbours.

When Jack went off to build other people's houses, his wife stayed home and took her time making ruffled curtains and remembering Jack. Took her time and stayed soft. She talked a little to the neighbours. She liked to go for walks by the river. She'd go to the library for books about rivers. She liked to read about flowers, too, and arrange them. As she cleaned the house she took time to enjoy the springiness of the feather duster, the little flurries of dust in the beams of the afternoon sun through the window, the ache that her Jack would be home soon. When they went to the shopping mall, she shopped and he carried. While he soaked in his bath, she barbecued their meals and served them up on the well-known platter. Jack and his wife talked about their day, what he had done and seen, what she had read and thought about. Dinner on the patio. A pretty picture.

A boring picture. The neighbours were ready to believe in something different. They knew the Sprats shared one task: washing the platter. The neighbours always knew whose turn it was.

Sometimes in the privacy of their kitchen Jack ate a little fat and his wife some lean. Then softly they would talk about their house, where they belonged, where they longed to be. Where they'd shaped and accommodated one another at their platter and in their bed. And they'd laugh at themselves. How he liked to go out and attract attention, though he didn't have to go—she would give him all he needed. How she fretted about him, though she didn't have to

73

—didn't he always come back to their beloved house? They laughed lightly with the mirror that showed them back their unfathomable contrast, fat and lean. As they breathed back and forth in sleep, it seemed the silent walls breathed with them.

One day it was Jack's turn to wash the platter and he wouldn't.

*No way*, said Jack.

All day she had dreamed about him, and now it was his turn to wash the platter.

*Later*, said Jack. He went off to the tavern to digest his meal in a different kind of attention. He was lean enough to get away with what he was doing.

She started to fret right away. But she was dreamy and clever enough to be able to put on a creative front. She left the platter where it was—at least he had carried it to the sink. With hammer ringing she boarded up both kitchen doors, the one to the living room and the one to the back porch. Of course she used only a few token nails. And as she worked she thought. The best way she knew to enjoy being fat was to have Jack beside her being lean. The next best way to enjoy being fat was to bake pies. She took what she would need, hammered up the last board with a flourish, and went to a neighbour's kitchen.

There she made two pies, one for the neighbour and one for herself. From the scraps of dough she made stick-figure shapes like the parts of Jack's body. When the parts were baked she joined them with gumdrops and decorated the whole cookie to the last detail of Jack's clothes and his half-serious smile. With a pat on its fragile bum she sent the cookie off toward the tavern. In its fragrant wake she blew a kiss.

A second neighbour came to share the pie and invite the two women to her kitchen, which was larger. And the three made pies and ate them. Out of the scraps of dough the neighbours made more stick-figure cookies, which they decorated to look like Jack, and sent off to the tavern with lewd gestures. Mrs. Sprat wished the cookies didn't walk so much like her husband.

More neighbours came by with what they needed, and all the women went together to the kitchen of the town hall. While Mrs. Sprat was fretting, the neighbours quickly turned out a few pies. Then they pressed the scraps together into a ball and rolled out the dough for cookies. As they did, strange thoughts spun in their heads, hopeful and vengeful thoughts. More and more dough they made, and how they pressed and rolled it! Brandishing knives, they

74

carved out body parts uncannily like Jack's. With licorice whips they bound the parts together. High-spirited, the women pushed the cookies roughly toward the tavern.

While Mrs. Sprat was fretting. She didn't like to see them enjoying themselves so much. But with Jack away so long, who did she have if not her neighbours? To cheer her up they fed her another pie. When she looked unwell they teased her—surely she hadn't eaten too much?—and carried her home on their shoulders. They stayed with her. They positioned their large bodies to protect her from the sight of her boarded-up kitchen. They helped her think of a better life.

She could travel and exhibit the well-known platter. If she needed time to get used to her new situation she could stay in town and bake pies to sell, and her neighbours would travel and exhibit the platter. They liked that idea. They would sell replicas of the platter with modern slogans on them. Surreptitiously they peeked between the boards into the kitchen. None of them had ever seen the platter up close. Mrs. Sprat listened to her neighbours making their own plans in her house at such a time. She wanted no part of this kind of friendship. She tuned their voices out. Smiling to herself she pictured Jack in the tavern, ready to speak the nonsense that she loved.


There he was with an admiring eye on himself reflected behind the bar, everyone around him ready to listen, when the first cookie Jack came into the tavern looking as if it were ready to speak. Jack couldn't remember which way the mirror was. In his confusion half the attention he so craved slipped away to his cookie self. More cookies came in, with expressions he didn't like at all. He was dizzy seeing himself coming and going. There seemed to be a joke about his body that he didn't feel part of. Still more cookies came in, or were they the old ones mirrored and re-mirrored? Jack could hardly remember his clothes. Or the sound of his voice—the cookies' silence was getting the attention now.

Surrounded by himself he is afraid. What is a lean man without his fat woman to be soft with? And how is his fat woman getting along? With no clean platter how can she eat? How can she eat without him there? He himself has forgotten to eat. He has forgotten her slow smile, and remembers only the ominous sound of her hammering. He wants to go home, where he owns the mirror and it shows him himself. It shows the two of them. He misses her fretting where he can see her. Oh, how he'll feed her, comfort her!

He comes back ready to wash the platter, and finds their beloved kitchen boarded up. Hearing the neighbours voices he works quietly. Carefully he removes the boards from the door to the back porch, and his hope rises at her message of the easy nails. He repairs the wounds in the walls. He washes the floors and counters and shelves. The platter has dried hard in the dusty sink, but Jack is undaunted. He clears the rusty water out of the pipes. He goes out to buy detergent, for what's left is stuck to the old container. He fills the sink with suds and soaks the platter. The old scouring pad is crusted with mold so he goes out again to buy a new one. Even from the store he hears the voices of the neighbours in his house, plotting, while he longs for the way she laughs when the two of them are quiet. Her laughter purling up through all her flesh.

Thick as a bramble hedge the neighbours surround her. Scheming, cackling, protecting her so that she doesn't hear him. But she senses the warm dishwater in their kitchen, and she longs to be beside him, hands in the sink together.

He takes his time with the platter, scrubs it gently. He senses her ears straining toward the kitchen and his ears strain toward her, back and forth. And their yearning sets the walls swaying and the nails loosening and falling out of the boards.

A shout. One word shouted in her voice, hitherto so acquiescent. One reverberating shout. The platter slips from her husband's hands. The house itself collapses onto the stupefied neighbours.

Lean Jack, fat wife, and the kitchen sink, upright amid the flat debris. A bit of kitchen left to mend the platter in.


The Sprats have a mystery now, which fascinates them. What was the word she had shouted? Stop? Don't? Help? Love? Did she call out Jack's name in her distress? Or a name for herself?

The mystery sustains them, for their life has changed. Jack never goes to the tavern now, though he misses planning to come home to her. She misses the sweet uncertainty of fretting. When they rebuilt their house together she took her turn on the roof, where the neighbours, licking their wounds, could see how scared she was. Together the Sprats made curtains, he grim and visible in the window as he learned. Now they cook and eat indoors. To protect the platter they use it only for display, on a low shelf behind the dining room door.

For, like everyone else, they have a dishwasher. Going to work together, keeping house together, it seems they are far busier now for sharing. True to the custom that couples, in time, resemble one another, Jack has become less lean now and his wife less fat. Anything to withstand these troubled times.

# Twinkle, Twinkle, Little Star,
# The International Anthem

*Up above the world so high,*
*Like a diamond in the sky*

We, the innocent nation—how long did we continue to sing before we realized our star was gone? The song, our beloved anthem. Our diamond star, the hub of the sky.

Once we were secure in its steadfastness. We sang softly to it as we bent to sew fine seams. We sang as we set our dough to rise, and the fragrance rose up with our voices. How long had our star been gone?

Each women's nation had a diamond star. Each nation believed their own unchanging star kept the sky turning. From their separate, star-determined paths the nations regularly met and celebrated. Each sang their variation of the Twinkle song, a simple song, a simple trust. Each nation's separate motto was, *One anthem, one accord.*

One nation liked to sing so much they had a verse for every star in the sky. One nation sang to the artificial diamonds they produced in honour of their star. Another sang to the coloured lights they had invented. These nations must have thought we lived in a dark age. For though we, too, were scientific, and generous in spirit, we sang faithfully to our tiny diamond in the sky. Oh, for the innocent days when it still was up there! One nation sang to their eyes, that gazed upon their star. Another, to their star's reflection in their rivers. In this multiplicity our song was classic. When our life seemed dreary we remembered our pride.

How to maintain that pride in the face of our secret shame, the disappearance of our diamond star perhaps at one of the very moments we were singing to it?

*How I wonder what you are!*

79

Our wondering became an urgent question. What was up there now at the hub of the sky? Our experts on negative spaces their fields of knowledge Swiss cheese, lace, and graves—concurred that what they saw up there was less like a diamond than a hole. And yes, if we aimed our telescopes precisely we could see, more clearly than we would have liked, the result of our heedlessness exposed by moonlight. We could see what might be taken for a hole. Not a jagged hole but round, worn smooth, as if it had been there for a long time.

We blamed ourselves. We who had sung to our star, our diamond, even as we bent to sweep or tidy, who had sung as if our singing kept it up there, had we really known it? Perhaps our star had changed, and our song was no longer right for it. Perhaps it had twisted itself out of its setting to spin off and search for a different kind of song. Or perhaps, despairing, it had disintegrated into stardust, leaving us bereft. How long had we sung to our diamond star, not knowing it was gone?

We would simply find the diamond and put it back where it belonged. But where to look? Surely it couldn't be concealed among us without shining or somehow showing itself. As we stood there agreeing not to search, some of us nevertheless cast around meaningful glances. Could our star have strayed among the neighbouring nations? Best not to ask or they might guess our shame. Still, the more zealous among us got as far as the border before the rest of us stopped them with the force of reason. And of shame.

The *accord* of our motto, which had held through shock and shame, now splintered into speculation. Some of us wanted to replace the diamond star, though we couldn't agree on anything that might suffice. And would it be a replacement only in practical terms, of filling the hole, or in allegiance as well? And whatever we found, how would we put it up there? Some of us considered the very idea of a solution heartless: our loss itself was an experience to appreciate in all its sadness. Some were uneasy about leaving the hole unstoppered even briefly. The sun could occupy it and deprive us of our nights, our still-beautiful nights with their rich mystery. Or the moon creep in with its inconstant leadership. If the hole remained open, what might come out of it? The anger of the sky? The tears?

Perhaps the sky had betrayed us, forcing our diamond loose as if it were a mere irritation. Some of us wanted to send up rockets to pierce the treacherous sky. Some of us boycotted the sky by looking away, though we diminished only ourselves. With our burgeoning differences we hardly dared to wonder. When one of us, out of habit, said *I wonder...*, others would interrupt with a sharp *yes* or *no*, so no one would panic for an answer. We feared we might never again agree.

At least when we celebrated with the other nations we felt as one. We held up our heads and sang the old song anyway, our urgent nostalgia giving it spirit. But when the other nations sang, robustly or demurely as they always had, to us their singing seemed complacent and our song rang doubly false. *Twinkle, twinkle, little star*—we didn't mean that any longer. With nothing, literally nothing, to sing to we would rather have remained silently anxious. Nights seemed to come more often with their melancholy.

To shield our pain we adopted euphemisms. When we played cards we called our now ignominious red suit *bits* or *pointy things*, but our luck failed us. We said *baseball square*, and had to look at it obliquely to correct the meaning. When we called our starfish *bumpyskins*, they drew in their tentacles and shuddered. We didn't have to forbid the use of the old words. We were loyal, and none of us held to them. But uttered innocently by the other nations chatting between anthems, those words became obscene to us.

Obscene and naive, as seemed their singing now. In our misfortune we turned to gossip. Which nations might have lost their diamonds without knowing? In whose skies were the diamonds firm, in whose were they shifting? We didn't like our graceless selves. We decided to keep private from the other nations. We would refuse to celebrate until, one night, we would look up and see the sky once more intact with our diamond star.

When the other nations didn't see us they seemed to take no notice. Perhaps they realized our disgrace, that we no longer sang. Perhaps they felt sorry for us. Perhaps they knew that before we could show ourselves we had to come up with an honest anthem and, before that, something to sing to. They left us alone with our affliction. With our task.

Which we evaded. We thought of other holes. The mythical hole through the earth that led to China. Why couldn't our nation, now symbolically connected, find that hole? Or dig it? And the hole in the bottom of the sea, source of the rollicking anthems of underwater nations. Couldn't we sing with them, to our hole in the sky?

At grand moments some of us called our hole a void, an ultimate possibility. Beyond the hole there could be a mirror sky, or

81

another earth, with oceans. A few of us talked of ascending through the hole in glory—such glory could be the subject of an anthem—but the rest of us held onto their skirts and kept them safe. To most of us our hole was just a hole, with the shabbiness that word implied. What was true besides our shame was our uncertainty.

And fear. Starless, diamondless, with a hole the hub of the sky, were we at liberty or drifting? Would the sky, now free, stop turning? Would it undulate instead? Or swoop? Was the hole vast? Would it draw ships into it? The salt we threw over our shoulders? Ourselves, and to what purpose?

We shouted these fears one after another up to our hole in the sky, and the sky stayed firm. We shouted them again, louder and louder, till they echoed against the sky, and the sky stayed firm. We shouted out all the fears we'd ever had, our pain, our disagreements, till the din abated and there were no fears left. Beyond our fears were other, rudimentary feelings, not ready to be told. So we neither spoke nor sang. Patient until the heavy silence lessened our shame, our need for an anthem, our old pride in our diamond star. Until the silence itself lightened to a kind of peace. And we went quietly about our days and nights, and little bits of song came softly to us.

We found ourselves once more among the neighbouring nations. We were giggling. Though unprepared we were about to sing. What came out was the fine, familiar tune. Each of us sang as we did at home, a few words now and then out of our individual humour, wistfulness, determination. Quietly, for as well as singing we were listening to each other.

This was our anthem now, our song of mystery and reverberation. We sang it gently, strongly, gently. Steadfast within our nation, each of us on a separate uncertain path, we followed into the night the bits of song we cast ahead.

# III

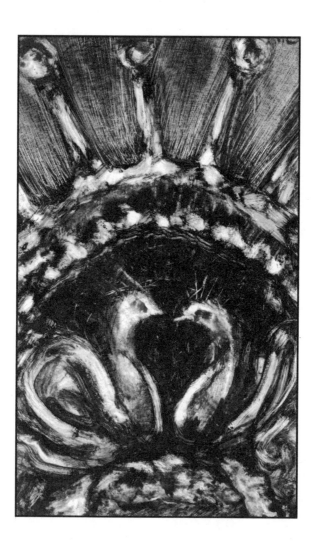

# Cinderella and All the Slippers:
# The Story of the Story

It sometimes happens that a kingdom loses its sense of romance and falls into lassitude. The present story, a Cinderella story, found itself in such a kingdom.

The story woke inside a tulip in the palace garden, woke slowly from the vast, ancestral dream that was the source of all Cinderella stories. It savoured its new awareness. Here it was, one of the greatest, most romantic stories of all time. It peeked out over the garden to make sure its tulip was the prettiest colour. The tulip showed how gracefully it could sway, then held itself straight. Fast as a secret, the honour of the story's presence passed from flower-bed to flower-bed. In a wave of admiration, or so it appeared to the story, the flowers straightened their stems and elbowed the weeds into bowing down.

The story took notice of the weeds. And when it perched in the crown of a passing peacock and rode to the palace in style, it took notice of the very shabby red carpet. With the kingdom's need so clear, what better place for a story such as itself to shine? The peacock strutted through the palace at the story's will, and the story looked for its characters. The king sat in the ballroom looking at the dusty floor. The prince kept himself turned away in thought no matter how provocatively the peacock displayed its train before him. Restless, the story sprawled instead on the articulated back of a butterfly. Fluttering back and forth over the river the story admired its butterfly's changing reflection. And on the riverbank by a hazel tree it found the mother and child.

Cinderella stories were well known. Many mothers dreamed idly, and their daughters less idly, of a happy ending for themselves. But this mother believed there could be no ending without a story first. To fortify her daughter for the demands of such a story she called her Cinderella from the outset. She taught her pride in a name that had come from the French and implied the purity of ashes. She taught her the dignity of household work done well and the opportunity to reflect while doing it. Together they sat sorting their daily lentils and throwing the bad ones out the window for the birds. *Remember to distinguish good from bad*, the mother said. *Be patient. And think of your mother, who taught you.*

The story was taken aback. Such seriousness had no place in a romantic story. At the same time the story had faith in the mother. She was the character to whom it felt it could make itself known. It was ready to flutter in her face to the end of the butterfly's strength if need be. But the mother quickly understood the sign. The colours of the butterfly reminded her of the slippers her own mother had taught her to make, and she knew it was time to pass the tradition on to her daughter. As they sewed and embroidered, the mother retold the old Cinderella stories. Slippers were once made of gold or fur or glass, she said. Princes captured them by coating the palace steps with sticky substances such as pitch or honey. Word of the story's presence spread, and slipper making was revived throughout the kingdom.

The story loved to wriggle in among the slipper silks and listen to the mother talk. But as Cinderella made beautiful things and turned beautiful herself, the story's romantic spirit faltered. It longed to see Cinderella in rags. Fortunately, in such a famous story, the characters knew what to do, and it felt it could leave them in charge of the plot. The story itself retreated among the flowers to restore its spirit. And to avoid the sadness of what was about to happen.

The mother died and was buried under the hazel tree beyond the garden. Every day Cinderella visited the grave with her father and felt comforted. She liked to hear the birds that perched in the tree and to catch sight of an old woman who sometimes visited the grave. But Cinderella was soon left to herself. Her father, missing his wife's calm wisdom and assuming all women to be the same, married again in haste.

The father's new wife thought tradition was just a hoax to hold you back from getting what you wanted. She believed in capitalism, that anyone could marry a prince if she knew how to capitalize on her good features. Dismissing the story as superstition, she married to give her daughters a chance at a prince. For the prince in this kingdom had recently come of age. Any day the king would announce a festival at which the prince would choose a bride.

The new wife also believed in democracy. She encouraged

her daughters to interfere however they could to minimize any unfair advantage Cinderella might have, her name, her beauty, her character. The daughters knew of the different outcomes of past Cinderella stories. They were mad with curiosity to know which fate would be theirs: to be blinded, to marry a minor member of the court who was probably an old man, or to be forgotten and repent in obscurity. To distract themselves from these alternatives they tormented Cinderella, and thus went along with the story.

They made Cinderella stay in her traditional place by the hearth so that she would always be dirty, in keeping with her name. She was prepared for that. She would sit there sorting lentils, good from bad, as she had learned from her mother. The stepsisters would throw the lentils right into the cold hearth. Unperturbed, Cinderella would separate the lentils from the delicate ashes that vanished between her fingers, and reflect—there was good and bad, and ephemeral, as well. The one torment that got to her was an original creation of the stepsisters'. Wherever Cinderella was cleaning, the stepsisters would set up a little tea table. With a great smacking of lips they would eat the fancy cakes they had bought themselves at the market. Then they would wipe their sticky hands on Cinderella's ragged skirt. Cinderella, always hungry, would be dizzy with bending and the smell of vanilla.

The story liked to nestle in the sugarbowl in the midst of this action. It was well aware there were harsher torments in other Cinderella stories. But the style of this torment was in keeping with the refined story from the French court, with which the present story liked to identify.

In her distress Cinderella looked to her father, but he was rarely there. To make his new family happy he stayed away most of the time earning money so that he could bring home dresses and ribbons, the kinds of things he assumed women wanted. He was thankful to the story for this role to retreat into. He wished he knew what to buy for his own daughter, but she was so beautiful he couldn't bring himself to ask.

The story had mixed feelings about Cinderella. If her beauty was so beneficial to the story's image, how could it have such a bad effect on its spirit? All it could think of was, what if Cinderella got all the attention and the story itself were ignored? The story went back to the flowers, where it could feel romantic again. Here it felt superior, as well, because of its complex plot. But the flowers were not impressed. They budded, bloomed and died, and whatever the story thought of itself, it would have the same fate.

The story removed itself from the disrespectful flowers to take comfort among the slippers, which were more its style. Cinderella had made pair after pair for her stepsisters to wear to the festival. The story might have hovered forever admiring such an array, had the slippers not seized the opportunity to make their concerns known. The longer the festival was delayed and the more plentiful slippers became, the more painful it would be when only one of them was chosen for the grand finale. Furthermore they felt that one of their kind should rightfully be the heroine. Cinderella was pretty enough, but now and historically, whatever they were made of—filigree, ermine, crystal—slippers were far more ornate than she. As long as she was working on them they praised her skill. They basked in the thought that museums might bid for them. Still, the slippers suspected they would fare badly in the present story as very minor characters and threatened to boycott it unless they appeared in the title. The story retreated from the growing number of insensitive characters to a nondescript tulip in an unfamiliar garden. If anyone knew where it was, it would at least seem dramatic in its solitude.

At last the festival was announced. The stepsisters went out to watch the palace garden being weeded and the new red carpet being laid. They felt the desire to step up preparations at home. By this time they had plenty of slippers to choose from so they made other work for Cinderella. They became fussy about their food and spilled their tea or left their dirty cups in odd places. They made her pick out the blue embroidery from one pair of slippers and replace it with green, and pick out the green from another pair and replace it with blue. Cinderella lost pleasure in her work. She harboured the malicious hope that the slippers would show up the stepsisters' plainness and people would laugh. She had no time to visit her mother's grave, or see the birds in the hazel tree or the old woman whose distant presence comforted her. She vowed not to forgive the story for letting that happen. How much pain was a story worth?

The slippers sided with the stepsisters, and the story, from its sugarbowl, sided with the slippers. Though on principle the story abhorred the idea of pain, Cinderella's case was different. Real suffering was a necessary contrast to a happy ending. If the story's image might have been enhanced by a show of courage, it would have come out of its provisional tulip and enjoyed seeing Cinderella ugly in distress.

Cinderella spent the day of the festival dressing the stepsisters and arranging their hair. When they were satisfied with themselves in the mirror, they saw their chance. Too excited to eat, they flounced up to Cinderella with their little cakes and squashed them against her back, where the icing stuck at the spot she couldn't reach no matter how she twisted.

*Get out! Get out! I want to be rid of you!* She dashed the sugarbowl onto the hearth. The stepsisters jumped and screeched in triumph. They had made Cinderella like themselves. Worse than themselves, for they never smashed things. They would have tittered all the way to the festival. But their mother shocked them into a semblance of dignity by pointing out there was only one prince between them.

Cinderella attacked the hearth. With her fingernails she dug at a large stone until she worked it loose. She felt the satisfaction of its weight in her hand. She was just about to heave it out the doorway when the stranger, the old woman she had seen near her mother's grave, came in. The woman spoke gently until Cinderella put down the stone and cried in her arms. Cinderella slept a little. Then the fairy godmother, for that's who it was, bathed her in the river. And there was Cinderella in a shimmering dress and slippers her mother had once made. She was shy at her reflection in the river there was a difference between making something beautiful and wearing it herself. The pumpkin coach was ready with its small, mouse-coloured horses. The fairy godmother sent her off to the festival in the care of a lizard coachman.

As Cinderella approached the palace the other guests were on their way home. When she caught sight of them her coach, horses, and coachman vanished. In rags once more, she hid behind a thicket by the road as the guests passed. She heard them wonder about the flash of golden coach they thought they had seen. But they soon went back to grumbling. For the prince had met them at the gate, thanked them for coming, and announced his regrets. He felt that before he was ready to choose a bride he would have to make a thorough study of slippers and take a stand on an important traditional issue. He was sure they would understand.

Cinderella crept home the long way and reflected on her strange day. How angry she'd been, then how peaceful with her fairy godmother. She thought of the lizard coachman with his cool, unblinking eye and flickering tongue, how his luxurious indolence had mesmerized her into silence. She remembered her reflection in the river and then in the window of the coach against the night sky. How grand, how dreamy, she had looked! Yes, she was well suited to her role in the story.

The king announced a second festival. The fairy godmother came to Cinderella with apologies. Perhaps pumpkins had been used too often and were no longer effective. This time she chose a vegetable marrow for a long, greenish-gold coach. She chose a frog as coachman. Once again Cinderella met the other guests grumbling on their way home——the prince would not relent. Cinderella pondered this. She reconsidered the opportunity she had just let go by. For she'd been fond of the small, bright-skinned frog coachman that kept leaping up from his seat. He had said to her in his bubbly, rumbling way, *I have my own story. It's called "The Frog Prince." If you take me home and throw me against the wall you'll break my spell.*

The present story happened to be in the vicinity and overheard the frog's offer. Avoiding the sight of Cinderella in her splendid clothes, the story was busy choosing a new household object to relax in, something sturdier than a sugarbowl though just as pretty, when it took in the implications of the frog's offer and felt the full force of the shock. Kidnapping! Violence! Gratified as the story had been when Cinderella showed her temper or was drawn to vulgar creatures, the threat of sabotage was of a much graver order. The story was chilled to realize how close it had come to losing its main character. Perhaps there had actually been stories like that, aborted stories, which no one remembered. To help itself forget this dreaded possibility, the story went on vacation up north. Thinking of itself as a gambler, it made up a kind of snowflake roulette. The idea was to attach itself to several different snowflakes in turn. If one of them fell exactly on the tip of the Pole, the story would be transformed into "The Snow Queen."

The story came back not necessarily in defeat but out of concerned curiosity. There was a rumour that the prince had gone off to the wars. The king was puzzled, for he wasn't aware of any wars the kingdom was waging. He continued to announce festivals, for he didn't know what else to do. He lay awake with his obsession. If you do away with tradition, what do you do away with next? Kings?

The story commiserated with the king, for it, too, had a stake in tradition. Fresh wars had no place in a romantic story. Worrying about them could disrupt the kind of dreams it liked to immerse itself in. These dreams might have been enhanced by the sight of the prince, but the story wasn't about to sully its image by chasing after him. Especially not for that Cinderella. The story draped itself over the smoothest jewel in the king's crown and there it stayed through the preparations for one festival after another.

Each time the stepsisters were turned away from the palace they became meaner, and Cinderella suffered more. They sought out the smallest lentils at the market to make her work more difficult. When they discovered she was feeding the birds, they killed them. Her father died, and she missed him as she had when he'd been alive Now the widowed stepmother had to be dressed for the festivals as well, for she, too, had her eye on the prince. In time, the hopes of all three waned and their meanness wore thin. They wandered around the house distracted and irritable. When they talked at all they muttered about the prince and despaired they would never marry. They paid no attention to Cinderella. She cooked for herself and mixed nettles into the leftovers she served them. She sent them to the festivals with colours mismatched and dirty linen trailing behind.

Cinderella herself had long stopped going to the festivals. Instead she persuaded her fairy godmother to visit with her, and together they created their own excitement. They thought of changing Cinderella's name or disguising her as one of the stepsisters, to force the story out of hiding. They thought of building a restaurant. They went as far as sketching some plans on a bed of smoothed-down ashes. People would gather there, and Cinderella and her fairy godmother would have friends and live normal lives as if they had never taken the story seriously. But they decided they were not so ambitious after all. Feet touching, they would sit before the hearth and watch the luxurious fire they had made for themselves. Sometimes they walked arm in arm by the river and talked about their childhoods, Cinderella's mother, or the fairy godmother's arthritis, which, since her powers were limited, ached as much as anyone else's. This way they got the story to show the pleasure of friendship between women.

In the absence of pain faith comes easy, and Cinderella began to believe in the story again. She prepared to be swept away by romance. Using pieces of the stepsisters' best clothes, she made dresses for herself to wear to the faraway places the prince would take her. She was thankful to the story for such a future to dream about.

But the bane of faith is boredom, and the story, still at the palace, lost faith in itself. All it ever expected was to float along unhampered and admired, oblivious to anyone it may have harmed. Yet so much had gone wrong. An essential character had absented himself without extending the courtesy of asking permission. Others had abandoned the romantic spirit just because they had been turned away from a few festivals. Cinderella and the fairy godmother took advantage of the story's good nature and mocked it. Did none of them think of posterity? Of the glory of being associated with a story that turned out well?

Even if its characters were fickle, the story was not about to give up on its own good name. It would devise a new ending, so spectacular that no one would remember the characters it had started with. An earthquake? An apocalypse? A quintuple messianic birth? No. All distasteful and irrelevant, not in keeping with the story's fanciful, avant-garde self. In search of a new perspective the story went off around the world to see what other Cinderella stories were making of themselves.

It found several with no slippers but a ring. Perhaps rings were less temperamental. One story had two stepmothers and six stepsisters. Another had poppyseeds, so tiny that the present story was embarrassed at the clumsiness of its lentils. There were very few fairy godmothers, though in one story a red calf helped Cinderella, in another, a blue bull. In the elegant oriental story there were buried fishbones and a cache of pearls. In exotic seas the story takes a break. Undulating among the angelfish it contemplates what it has learned. All these stories are preparing to turn out essentially like their predecessors. The present story is their kin. At heart it is a grand romantic, and that's how it wants to be remembered. It opts to uphold tradition. As the crow flies, the story returns to its kingdom.

Fortunately for the story, for it is now too weary to go searching, the prince comes galloping back. He has made his way through the ideological wars of the golden-slipper, fur-slipper, and glass-slipper believers. Slippers are pretty enough, but now he knows it is the spirit of slippers he cares for. Now he is ready for romance, ready to meet Cinderella, whose position has always been linked with his. He is ready to marry her with slippers and crown and care for her happily ever after.

He slows to a trot. As the story hops on, it slips unpleasantly in the horse's perspiration before latching onto a silver buckle on the harness. Trembling there the story wonders where to place itself to best experience its finale and at the same time protect itself from the wrath of all the unchosen slippers. It tries the prince's crown, his earring, the cuff of his sleeve but, sympathetic as the prince is, the story can't seem to secure itself. It feels ephemeral. Its awareness flickers. It casts about, but not a flower can hold it, nor a butterfly, nor a peacock, nor a peacock feather. Will it come to nothing, after all? *Too soon, too soon!* it longs to cry out. Oh, for a voice! No chance now of stealing the last scene, or even having a good cry. What about the kingdom, that needs its help

In his heart the prince saluted the fading story. Then he turned to the business at hand. There was Cinderella's house just beyond the garden. But he didn't feel like shaving. He got off his white horse. He searched in his saddle-bags for something to munch on but there was nothing. It was twilight, so he lay on the ground to sleep. When Cinderella went walking in the morning she would find him there and bring him breakfast.

Cinderella knew the prince was nearby. Once again she admired her finest slippers, which she had laid out in readiness long ago. When the story faded she put them away. She was tired of fussing over them, shaking out the dust and moving them around to protect them from strong light. She lay on the hearth, where the prince would find her in the morning and take her away. Though she wished he would leave the whole business for the weekend. She had just started spring cleaning, and wanted to finish her work.

And so the prince and Cinderella slept with the garden between them. They dreamed the same silent dream—he came softly toward the hearth, from a sea of slippers rescued her wrinkled foot and warmed it in his hands. Bright flowers between them, they dreamed this dream as if it had happened long ago.